DOC SAVAGE'S AMAZING CREW

William Harper Littlejohn, the bespectacled scientist who was the world's greatest living expert on geology and archaeology.

Colonel John Renwick, "Renny," his favorite sport was pounding his massive fists through heavy, paneled doors.

Lieutenant Colonel Andrew Blodgett Mayfair, "Monk," only a few inches over five feet tall, and yet over 260 pounds. His brutish exterior concealed the mind of a great scientist.

Major Thomas J. Roberts, "Long Tom," was the physical weakling of the crowd, but a genius at electricity.

Brigadier General Theodore Marley Brooks, slender and waspy, he was never without his ominous, black sword cane.

WITH THEIR LEADER, THEY WOULD GO ANYWHERE, FIGHT ANYONE, DARE EVERYTHING—SEEKING EXCITEMENT AND PERILOUS ADVENTURE!

Bantam Books by Kenneth Robeson

THE MAN OF BRONZE
THE THOUSAND-HEADED MAN
METEOR MENACE
THE POLAR TREASURE
BRAND OF THE WEREWOLF
THE LOST OASIS
THE MONSTERS
THE LAND OF TERROR
THE MYSTIC MULLAH
THE PHANTOM CITY
FEAR CAY
QUEST OF QUI
LAND OF ALWAYS-NIGHT
THE FANTASTIC ISLAND
MURDER MELODY
THE SPOOK LEGION
THE RED SKULL
THE SARGASSO OGRE
PIRATE OF THE PACIFIC
THE SECRET IN THE SKY
COLD DEATH
THE CZAR OF FEAR
FORTRESS OF SOLITUDE
THE GREEN EAGLE
THE DEVIL'S PLAYGROUND
DEATH IN SILVER
THE MYSTERY UNDER THE SEA
THE DEADLY DWARF
THE OTHER WORLD
THE FLAMING FALCONS
THE ANNIHILIST

THE ANNIHILIST

A DOC SAVAGE ADVENTURE

BY KENNETH ROBESON

THE ANNIHILIST
*A Bantam Book / published by arrangement with
The Condé Nast Publications Inc.*

PRINTING HISTORY
Originally published in DOC SAVAGE *Magazine December 1934*
Bantam edition published December 1968

*All rights reserved.
Copyright, 1934, by Street & Smith Publications, Inc.
Copyright renewed 1962 by The Condé Nast Publications Inc.
This book may not be reproduced in whole or in part, by
mimeograph or any other means, without permission.
For information address: The Condé Nast Publications Inc.,
420 Lexington Avenue, New York, N.Y. 10017.*

Published simultaneously in the United States and Canada

*Bantam Books are published by Bantam Books, Inc., a subsidiary
of Grosset & Dunlap, Inc. Its trade-mark, consisting of the words
"Bantam Books" and the portrayal of a bantam, is registered in the
United States Patent Office and in other countries. Marca Registrada.
Bantam Books, Inc., 271 Madison Avenue, New York, N.Y. 10016.*

PRINTED IN THE UNITED STATES OF AMERICA

Contents

Chapter I

THE POP-EYED DEAD

John Henry Cowlton was the first pop-eyed dead one. Cowlton was a young man who had inherited money, and the newspaper reporters, writing his obituary the next morning, called him a Park Avenue playboy. Cowlton was found in his penthouse gymnasium, and because the gym windows were open and it had been a cold night, his body was frozen only slightly less hard than a rock. There was no mark on John Henry Cowlton's athletic body. But there was a very peculiar thing wrong with his eyes.

John Henry Cowlton's eyes were protruding completely from their sockets, and for no good reason that the coroner could find. They were quite horrible, those eyes.

Everett Buckett was the second pop-eyed dead one. They found him in his limousine, which he drove himself. Buckett was a Wall Street operator whose machinations had sometimes moved others to call him "Old Bucket of Blood." He was worth upward of forty millions of dollars.

There was no mark on his body, but every one who saw his corpse noted the way the eyes stuck out. Not only was this horrible to look at, but it gave the undertaker considerable trouble.

Of course Everett Buckett's death was connected with that of John Henry Cowlton, on account of the eyes. But the catch was that there was no other connection between the two men, as far as any one knew. They had not even been acquaintances.

And certainly no one could connect "Nutty" Olsen with Everett Buckett, Wall Street wolf, and John Henry Cowlton, Park Avenue socialite.

Nutty Olsen was the next victim, and they found him in his cheap, filthy room with his eyes all a-pop. Nutty had been in numerous jails and he had a long police record; he was known as an utterly bad character. It was even suspected that he had murdered his mother because the old lady had once turned him over to the police. This had never been proved.

1

All of these deaths were in Manhattan.

The next one was in the Bronx. By this time, newspapers had started putting the pop-eyed deaths on the front page, and people who had nothing else to do were wondering if some new and mysterious disease might not have sprung up.

The Bronx victim was a lawyer, noted as a very honest man. He had a large family. They heard him screaming in his room. When they reached him, he was spread out on the floor with his eyes sticking out.

The tabloid newspapers began to turn handsprings. They ran big headlines; and the more timid citizens of New York began to look into mirrors frequently to see if anything was wrong with their eyes.

The thing was not a joke. A fifth and sixth man were found dead—one a comfortably fixed insurance man, the other a down-and-out hanger-on in a pool hall—and their eyes were not pleasant things to look at. The seventh was a professor in the city's largest university.

There was no conceivable connection between any of these men. But they all died with their eyes sticking out.

The police department, urged by the mayor, sent to Chicago for a specialist in strange diseases, for none of the victims showed the slightest mark on their bodies. The conservative New York papers became as wild as the tabloids. They did their best to worry every one.

Certain unnaturally timid persons began to go south to Florida earlier than they had intended. Others went to Europe. Those who had country homes paid them a visit. So far, it was only the timid who were worried. But before long, every one was to feel the terror of it.

They thought it was some new disease. They were wrong. Just how hideously wrong, no one had yet realized. The secret of the whole thing started coming out after what happened at the Association of Physical Health.

In the Association of Physical Health, there was a frosted glass inner-office door which bore the legend:

Dr. J. Sultman, President

Behind the door, a man yelled hoarsely, "I won't do it! No!"

There were scuffling sounds and a thump as if a chair had been upset. Rattling of the doorknob indicated some one was trying to get out.

In the big outer office, stenographers stopped typing. The flashy blonde on the phone switchboard ceased chewing gum and opened her lips.

The small man sitting in one of the leather chairs reserved for customers lowered his newspaper against his chest and looked over it, then shifted the paper so that his hands were concealed between it and his chest. The small man had long, oily hair and bleak blue eyes. His clothing was extremely conservative.

"Let me out of here, you damned fiend!" roared the voice back of the door.

Then the frosted glass panel broke with a jangling explosion. The man on the other side was beating it out with his fists, and when he had a large opening, he threw a light-brown topcoat over the jagged edges and vaulted through. He did not bother to recover his coat, but plunged toward the elevators, breathing heavily, horror on his face.

The man did not look like one accustomed to violent physical action. He was portly, with ruddy cheeks, and his head was almost bald. He had long-fingered, capable hands, which were also unusually smooth-skinned.

The small man with the newspaper stood erect hastily, let the paper fall, and showed an automatic pistol which it had hidden.

"Wait, brother!" he said.

The portly man looked at the gun, veered sharply to the left and slammed himself down in the shelter of a long leather divan.

"Help!" he roared at the top of his voice. "Police! Help!"

The small man's mouth twisted, giving his face a cast of extreme evil. He aimed at the divan and began shooting, the gun convulsing and jumping with each ear-shattering report.

Stenographers screamed; nurses began running; and the blonde telephone girl swallowed her gum and tried to crawl under her switchboard.

When the small man's automatic was empty, he snapped a fresh cartridge clip into the magazine with the skill of an expert gunman. Then he ran around behind the divan.

The portly man was a limp heap, leaking crimson in several places, for the bullets had driven through the leather and upholstery of the divan.

The small man shot once more, deliberately, and his victim's head jarred as a small blue hole appeared a little above the eyes. Then the killer ran for the stairway beside the elevators.

He reached the first stair landing. There he stopped, began to writhe about and shriek.

Between yells, the killer gnashed his own lips so that scarlet ran down over his chin and stained his necktie and shirt front. He doubled over as best he could, stamping his feet, slowly, then threw back his head.

When his head was back, the strange thing happening to his eyes first became apparent. It looked as if something behind the orbs was slowly forcing them out of their sockets.

The small man fell down on the landing and his gargling noises weakened until, before many seconds had passed, he was silent. He ceased to breathe, but his body still retained its grotesquely stiff posture.

His eyes were all but hanging out of their sockets.

There was only one flight of stairs to the street, and heavy feet pounded these, mounting. Two policemen appeared, hands on hip holsters, and saw the body of the man on the landing.

"I'll be damned!" gasped one officer, impressed by the dead man's popping eyes. "Whatcha know about that? The eighth one!"

They went on up the stairs and entered the big reception room of the Association of Physical Health. There was much excitement, one of the stenographers having fainted.

The two policemen shouted down every one, gave orders that nobody was to leave, and one took up a position at the elevators after ascertaining there was no back door. The other cop made a brief inspection of the portly man who had been shot to death behind the divan.

One of the dead man's arms was outflung, and the wrist was encircled by a shiny metal band which the policeman at first mistook for a wrist watch, only to learn, on closer inspection, that it held in place a round metal disk which bore an inscription that read:

Should anything happen to this man, notify Doc Savage.

"Hell's bells!" gulped the officer, and ran for a telephone.

The blonde operator was too nervous to put up a connection, so the policeman did it himself, fumbling clumsily with the board.

"Doc Savage speaking," came over the wire.

The voice which had answered was one so unusual that the officer was startled into momentary silence. There was a remarkable depth and power to the voice, a quality of capability which even the shortcomings of telephonic reproduction did not mask.

"There's a man dead here," said the policeman. "On his wrist is an identification tag asking that you be called if anything should happen to him."

"What is the number on the back of the tag?" Doc Savage asked.

The officer went over and examined the tag, finding a number he had overlooked the first time. Then he came back.

"Twenty-three," he said.

The policeman waited for some comment—then a bewildered expression overspread his flushed features. He absently put a finger up and rubbed an ear, as if that organ were playing him tricks.

He was hearing one of the strangest sounds ever to come to his attention. It was a weird trilling, this note, having a fantastic rising and falling cadence, yet adhering to no definite tune. It might have been the product of a faint wind through the cold spiles of an ice field, or it might have been the sound of an exotic tropical bird. The note ebbed away as mysteriously as it had arisen.

"I shall be there shortly," Doc Savage said, and there was no trace of emotion in his unusual voice.

The policeman hung up and breathed, "Whew! Something about that guy gets you, even over the telephone!"

The other cop, who had come over and heard the last of the conversation, demanded, "Who is this guy Doc Savage?"

The first officer looked dumfounded. "You ain't kiddin' me?"

"Oh, I've heard gossip about him," said the other. "But nothing first hand. What's the dope on him?"

"He's probably the most unusual bird alive," said the first officer. "He's the biggest and strongest man you ever saw. And he's a whiz! He can do anything. Electricity, chemistry, engineering, he knows all about 'em all."

"What's his business?" demanded the other.

The first policeman shrugged. "High adventure, I guess. He likes excitement. And he goes around getting people out of trouble. But what I mean, he tackles things on a big scale. He saves thrones for kings and stops wars. That's his calibre."

The cop who was asking questions said, "He has five birds who help him, hasn't he?"

"Yeah. Scientists, electricians and so on. Each one of the five is a topnotch specialist in some line."

The other policeman nodded at the body, then at the telephone. "How come you called him?"

"That identification disk——"

"I know. But that's business for Inspector Hardboiled Humbolt. He won't like it, your calling this Doc Savage."

"I don't give a damn," said the other officer. "This Doc Savage has done more good for the world than any other ten living men you can name. Yeah—any fifty you can name."

"Hardboiled Humbolt is gonna lay an egg because you called Savage," grunted the first cop. "You could call the president and the governor and the marines, and Hardboiled would still kick. He likes to run things."

"Let him lay the egg," snorted the other policeman.

They went out to stand guard. Down in the street, the caterwauling of a police siren was becoming louder.

The roadster had a long wheelbase, but it was not flashy and there was nothing particularly outstanding about its appearance. Only close inspection would have shown that the body was moulded of armor plate and the tires were filled with sponge rubber which would not be affected greatly by bullets. The glasswork was also of bulletproof construction, and the machine was fitted with apparatus for laying either smoke or gas screens.

Under the hood, a siren whined softly.

It was hard to say whether it was the whining of the siren or the appearance of the remarkable bronze man at the wheel which caused traffic to be parted with alacrity. The siren was the type reserved for police squad cars. Furthermore, the license plate consisted simply of three letters and a number—DOC 1.

More than a few persons on the streets recognized the bronze man. His picture was often in the newspapers; his name was mentioned even more frequently in the prints.

"Doc Savage," some one said, and there was a small stampede for the curb to get a glimpse of the bronze man.

The roadster was a large one, a car in which an ordinary large man would have seemed small. But the bronze man had the build of a giant, even in the open machine. Tremendous muscular strength was apparent in his cabled hands and in the vertical muscles in his neck, which were like hawsers coated with a veneer of bronze.

This bronze hue was the giant's motif throughout, his unusually fine-textured skin having a metallic hue imparted by long exposure to intense sunlight; his hair, straight and fitting like a metal skullcap, was of a bronze only slightly darker; the quiet brown of his business suit added to the symphony in metal.

Perhaps the eyes of the bronze man were the most impressive thing about him. They were weird, almost fantastic eyes, like nothing so much as pools of fine golden flakes continuously stirred by tiny winds. In them was a hypnotic, compelling quality.

The bronze man wore no head covering, and his eyes roved ceaselessly, seeming never to devote attention to the driving but rather to the streets through which the roadster passed. In spite of the seeming inattention, there was an expert ease about the way he drove.

He reached the building which housed the Association of Physical Health, drew to the curb and switched off the engine. Little more than the sudden death of the ammeter needle indicated the motor had stopped, so silently had it operated.

The bronze man drifted a metallic, muscle-cabled hand under the dash and touched a switch. Soft static crackle began coming from a radio loud-speaker. He brought a hand microphone to view.

"Monk—Ham," he said into the mike.

A voice that might have belonged to a small child came from the radio speaker.

"We're only a few blocks away, Doc," said this small tone.

"Ham with you?" Doc questioned.

"The shyster? Sure. He's along."

"Watch the outside of the building." Doc Savage directed quietly.

"Sure," said the child-voiced "Monk." "What do you know about this Association of Physical Health?"

"It is a concern which makes a business of giving physical examinations," the bronze man replied. "A physician named Janko Sultman is the president and principal owner."

Monk asked, "Any idea what this means, Doc?"

"None whatever," said the bronze giant, and switched off the radio transmitter-receiver equipment.

He could hear the murmur of puzzled voices as soon as he entered the building. A police medical examiner was inspecting the body of the man who had died, pop-eyed, on the stair landing. He bowed with marked deference when he saw Doc Savage.

"What killed him?" Doc Savage queried.

"I haven't the slightest idea," the medical examiner said

promptly. "It has me stumped. But he's like the other seven."

The bronze man said nothing, but knelt beside the dead man, his intention obviously being to make an examination.

There was a pounding of feet on the stairs, coming down from the second floor above. Doc Savage did not look around.

The newcomer was a burly man almost as large as Doc Savage. He had very large feet which were encased in canvas sneakers, and he walked as if his feet hurt him. His face gave the impression of being composed mostly of jaw.

He slammed a hand down on Doc Savage's shoulder. The hand was red and bony with a skin that looked as tough as rhinoceros hide.

"What the hell you doing?" he growled. "Get away from that body!"

The beefy man kept his hand on Doc Savage's shoulder as the bronze man stood erect. Then he shifted his grip to Doc Savage's arm. A slightly blank look overspread his bulldog face as he felt the hardness of the arm beneath. The next instant blankness became amazement as the bronze man plucked the hand off his arm, accomplishing the feat with apparent ease.

The burly man peered foolishly at his wrist, which bore pale grooves where the bronze man's fingers had reposed momentarily. He wriggled the fingers and seemed surprised that they functioned. Then he rumbled angrily, shook his arm up and down, and a shot-filled leather blackjack dropped into his hand. Evidently it had hung on a hook or rested in a shallow pocket in his sleeve.

"Tough guy, huh?" he growled.

"Don't be a fool, Hardboiled!" the medical examiner gulped. "This is Doc Savage."

"I know who he is," "Hardboiled" rumbled. "He's the guy who goes around mixing in other people's business, and guys who try to buck him have a funny way of disappearin'."

The medical examiner said, "Doc Savage has an honorary commission as inspector on the police——"

"Yeah, I know," Hardboiled growled. Then he leaned forward and tapped Doc's chest lightly with the end of his blackjack.

"Listen," he said. "I been intending to get around to you, only I've been too busy. I've heard a lot about you, and we know each other by sight. You may know I'm a tough cop. That's what the papers call me, damn 'em! I know you're the Man of Mystery, and I know people try to kill you and you do things to 'em and the law never hears about it. I don't like it. From now on, when anybody takes a shot at you, you call a cop and he'll handle it. Do it like anybody else does."

"In other words, have the police fight my battles?" Doc asked.

"Call it what you want," Hardboiled scowled. "There's laws to take care of crooks. And another thing: behave yourself and you won't have any battles to fight."

Doc asked dryly, "You have a faint suspicion I am a crook? Is that it?"

Hardboiled glared. "When I have suspicions, they're not faint!" he yelled. "I come out with 'em."

Doc said, "Suppose you come out with them now."

The beefy inspector's leather sap swung for emphasis.

"I think you do things outside the law!" Hardboiled roared. "That makes you subject to arrest. There are laws to punish criminals. And don't feed me that hokum about them not being punished in this day, because they are. Let the law take its course."

Doc said, "No one is disputing that."

Hardboiled put out his jaw. "I've heard that you set yourself up as judge, jury and penitentiary, all in one," he rapped. "Now that stuff don't go. You make one slip, and I'll clap your pants in the holdover so quick your head'll swim! If there's any one needs arresting in this town, that's my job. I do it. And I don't stand for anybody meddling with my job."

Doc murmured without expression, "Very clear."

Hardboiled got his jaw out farther. "Now I want civil answers to plain questions out of you. There has been two murders here, one of them the eighth in a damned mysterious chain of deaths that's beginning to get everybody all bothered."

"I see," Doc said.

"Go upstairs and take a look at that other body," Hardboiled directed. "Maybe you can identify it."

The medical examiner managed to work close to Doc Savage's side as the bronze man mounted the stairs.

"This Hardboiled is a character," he said. "He would insult the president. He's a leather-skinned cop of the old school, and he's been doing wonders at cleaning up Manhattan since they put him in charge. He's got a phobia for sticking to the letter of the law where police duties are concerned."

"I have been following Hardboiled's record," Doc Savage said quietly. "The man is just what Manhattan needed."

The examiner chuckled. "Hardboiled was canned by a previous administration for knocking the mayor down when they got in a quarrel over one of the mayor's friends breaking the speed limit. He's some character. His feet always hurt him. Maybe that's what makes him so grouchy."

Hardboiled Humbolt strode over to the body of the portly, bald man who had been shot to death and demanded of Doc Savage, "Who is he?"

"His name," the bronze man said, "was Leander Court."

"What was his business?" Hardboiled asked.

"He was a scientist and surgeon."

"How'd he hook up with you?"

The bronze man's flake-gold eyes seemed to acquire strange lights. "What do you mean?"

"How come he was wearing an identification tag asking that you be called if anything happened to him?" boomed Hardboiled.

"That, I shall not answer," Doc Savage said.

Hardboiled glared. "Say, didn't that lecture I just gave you take effect? You coöperate with me, or else you get in some trouble!"

He shook his sap down out of his sleeve.

The medical examiner yelled, "You're making an unmitigated fool out of yourself, Hardboiled!"

Hardboiled scowled and growled, "I don't like the methods of Doc Savage and I don't give a damn who knows it, and he's gonna answer my questions. There's some motive behind this killing, and I want to know what it is. I want to know why the other seven were killed."

"I can assure you," Doc Savage told him, "that I have not the slightest idea why Leander Court was killed, or the other seven, either."

"All right," snapped Hardboiled. "Now, why was he wearing that identification disk?"

Doc Savage ignored the question. "Just exactly what happened here?"

The medical examiner, who was embarrassed by the attitude which Hardboiled Humbolt had taken, said, "The dead man, Leander Court, arrived about an hour ago, according to the reception girl. He said he had an appointment with Janko Sultman, the president of the Association of Physical Health, and she directed him to Sultman's office.

"He was in there some time. Then he began yelling stuff about not doing something, and demanding to be let out. He broke the glass out of the door and climbed through. Then the man dead on the staircase downstairs shot him."

"When did the man downstairs appear?" Doc Savage interjected.

"Shortly after Leander Court arrived," said the examiner. "It looks as if the man followed Court here."

The bronze man nodded. "Then what?"

"After he shot Court, the man fled," explained the examiner. "He ran down the stairs, got to the first landing and had some kind of a fit, and died. That's as near as we can reconstruct it."

Doc Savage waved at the office. "Who was Leander Court yelling at before he broke out of the office?"

"That," said the medical examiner, "is a mystery."

"What do you mean?"

"There was nobody in the office."

Doc Savage swung over to the door and glanced through the jagged aperture where the frosted glass panel had been broken out. The office beyond was plainly furnished, the opposite wall being perforated with one window, and there was certainly no one inside. He tried the door. It resisted his efforts.

"The lock is peculiar," said the examiner. "It is a spring affair that has to be unlocked from either side with a key."

Doc Savage questioned, "You are sure no one left the office during the excitement?"

"They would have had to climb out," said the examiner. "Some one would certainly have noticed."

The bronze man glanced through the door again. The window was fitted with a substantial lock, and this was fastened. No one could have left by that route.

"Very mysterious," Doc Savage said.

"Not any more mysterious than your not wantin' to tell us why Leander Court wore that identification tag," Hardboiled Humbolt interjected sourly.

"Vot t'ings is happen here?" a strange voice demanded loudly.

Chapter II

THE MYSTERY QUEST

The man who had spoken was a bulky fellow, with upstanding, frizzled hair and a ludicrously small mustache. He wore an exceptionally loud checked suit which, however, seemed entirely in keeping with his unruly hair.

"You pol-eezmans, vot you do here?" he demanded. Then he glimpsed the body of Leander Court and gulped, "Dot man, who shot him?"

Hardboiled Humbolt shouldered forward and demanded, "Who the heck are you?"

The officer at the elevator called, "He said he was Janko Sultman, the president of the Association of Physical Health. I thought I'd better let him in."

Doc Savage asked abruptly, "Sultman, why did Leander Court come to see you?"

Janko Sultman looked puzzled. He made a tripod of the thumb and two forefingers of one hand, then reached up and absently massaged the top of his head.

"Leander Court," he murmured. "I am sorry, gent-eelmans, but dod name I not hear before. Never."

"Ever see him before?" the bronze man asked, and indicated dead Leander Court.

Sultman shook an emphatic, "Never!"

Hardboiled Humbolt, scowling at Doc Savage, monopolizing the questioning, strode forward so that he was between the bronze man and Janko Sultman.

"The telephone girl says Leander Court came in and said he had an appointment with you and was to wait in your private office," Hardboiled rumbled.

"Dot mystifies me," said Sultman. "Der man I have never seen before, believe you me."

Hardboiled shifted his sneaker-clad feet as if they hurt him, and said loudly, "Nobody seems to know a thing around here—except you." He glared at Doc Savage.

The bronze man nodded at the door from which the frosted glass was broken. "Mind if I try something?"

"Some of this snappy scientific detective stuff I hear you're so good at?" Hardboiled growled.

"Something like that," Doc admitted.

"All right," Hardboiled told him. "But before you start, let's get one thing straight."

"What?"

"You're under technical arrest on a charge of concealing evidence," said Hardboiled.

Every one except Doc Savage looked extremely surprised, and the bronze man asked quietly, "Just what sort of evidence am I hiding?"

Hardboiled jabbed a hand at plump Leander Court's bullet-riddled body. "Why is this guy wearing that identification disk?"

Doc Savage, seeming not to hear the question, said, "Let's look over the office where Leander Court waited."

Hardboiled swore, growled, "You're gonna find I'm not a healthy guy to kid along, big fellow," and led the way into the office from which Leander Court had smashed his way.

From a pocket, Doc Savage drew a small metal canister which had a perforated top. He twisted the lid so that the perforations were open, pepperbox fashion. Next, he pulled the shades over the locked window, causing gloom to descend upon the room. Outside, it was late afternoon of the first chilly day of fall.

Tilting the container, Doc Savage shook it. Liquid flame seemed to pour out and settle to the floor. The stuff was a powder which glowed like phosphorus.

Settling upon the floor, the stuff ceased to glow, except for certain spots which bore the shape of footprints.

The tracks showed where a man—they were unmistakably a man's footprints—had come into the office and occupied a chair. From the chair they led to a stand which held a telephone, and from the telephone back to the door. From telephone stand to door they were farther apart, as if the man who made them had been running wildly.

Doc Savage lifted the telephone receiver, listened a moment and replaced it on the hook.

"An outside line which does not go through the switchboard," he said. "That explains it. Leander Court was waiting here when he got a call. He became excited, cried out, and burst open the door in order to get out of the office."

"Nuts!" said Hardboiled Humbolt. "No man could be started off yelling by a telephone call."

Doc Savage replaced the metal canister in a pocket.

Hardboiled pointed and demanded, "What is that stuff, anyhow?"

"A powder which fluoresces, or glows, when exposed to the air," Doc Savage explained. "The slightest disturbance, by shifting the particles which compose the powder, causes them to expose new surfaces to the air, which in turn glow."

"But what made the tracks appear?" persisted the tough sleuth.

"The weight of Leander Court as he walked over the rug compressed the fibres," Doc elaborated. "Those fibres are still straightening, although by only microscopic degrees. But the movement is enough to disturb the powder, causing it to glow and mark the footprints."

"Well damn me!" Hardboiled growled. "I thought they had you overrated."

There was a spanking sound from the window. Glass particles geysered like tiny jewels.

Janko Sultman, president of the Association of Physical Health, bawled out loudly and hideously and fell to the floor. A wriggling red stream came out of his frizzled hair, puddling on the carpet.

Hardboiled Humbolt jumped fully a foot in the air, roared "Somebody shot 'im!" and ran for the window. He banged the panel up, leaned out, a hand fishing under his coat.

The gun he brought out was not the regulation service revolver, but a lean-snouted .22-calibre target pistol. He balanced this in a hand as his eyes roved the street.

"Car going down the street," he growled. "But the shot wasn't fired from the street, and the gunman hasn't had time to get to a car."

"What kind of a car is it?" Doc Savage questioned.

"Gray coupé," snapped Hardboiled. He hauled back out of the window, holstering his unusual weapon and bounded for the door. "You stay here, Savage!" he yelled. "You're still under arrest!"

Hardboiled plunged out through the door, taking ungainly leaps as if he were traveling on a hot surface. His gait and the canvas sneakers which he wore indicated he must have a bad case of corns.

Doc Savage was at the window, and he watched steadily for some moments. Then he backed away, stood over Janko Sultman and looked at the small round hole which the bullet had made in the window. It was on a line with the top of the building across the street.

"Strange there was no sound of a shot," said the medical examiner.

The bronze giant did not reply, but bent over and parted Janko Sultman's frizzled hair. Then he slapped Sultman's face with sharp, stinging force.

Sultman groaned, stirred, and shortly afterward was sitting up, his hands making aimless gestures. His eyes were cloudy.

"Boke," he mumbled thickly.

"Who is Boke?" Doc Savage asked.

The cloud went out of Janko Sultman's eyes and he held his head with both hands.

"Joke," he groaned. "I say dot bullet no joke. I guess you not understand right."

"Why should anybody try to shoot you?" Doc Savage asked sharply.

Sultman held his head and wailed, "I do not know, and dot is the truth, sure enough!"

Doc Savage went out into the reception room without saying anything, and found fresh excitement had arisen, with two of the stenographers screaming hysterically and the blonde telephone girl telling every one loudly that she was through.

"No telling who will get shot next," she wailed. "I'm through with this place! I'm quitting!"

Doc Savage went to the elevator and a policeman stopped him, saying, "I'm sorry. Hardboiled ordered you kept here."

The bronze man nodded, and roamed with apparent aimlessness over the offices. He peered into numerous small rooms where patients were examined, passed nurses and physicians without a word.

Down in the street, police sirens were wailing.

Doc Savage entered a washroom, closed the door and opened the tiny window. It gave into an air shaft. There was no door at the bottom of this, and no fire escape. The bronze man slid outside, negotiating the small aperture with a startling ease.

Had there been a hundred observers, fully ninety-nine of them would have sworn that not even a cat could climb the sheer wall. But the metallic giant went up in uncanny fashion, supported by the corded strength of his fingers and the shallow grooves between the bricks.

Reaching the top, he traveled over rooftops until he found a skylight, below which an artist painted. The artist, surprised, made a long smear on his painting as a giant man of metal smashed the skylight and dropped lightly at his side. While the artist stared, open-mouthed, the bronze man walked out.

Coming to life, the artist yelled, "Hey, I'll give you a hundred dollars to pose for me!"

There was no answer, and the artist, racing out, found no one. He returned, grumbling disgustedly, to stare at his picture, which was a partially completed study of a Herculean male figure supporting a certain well-known automobile. It was an advertising poster.

"What a model that fellow would have made," the painter groaned.

A uniformed patrolman loitered beside Doc Savage's roadster where it was parked in the street. His manner showed plainly that he had been posted there to watch the car. He twirled his club and walked around and around the machine, scrutinizing it closely. It had dawned on him that the car was no ordinary stock vehicle.

From behind him—from a door somewhere, it seemed—a harsh voice called, "Never mind the car! Go down and help the boys look for that gunman!"

The officer saluted briskly and departed. He thought he had recognized the tone as belonging to Hardboiled Humbolt. He rounded a corner, took a few paces—and came face to face with Hardboiled Humbolt in person.

"Dang it!" exploded the patrolman. "How'd you get here?"

"Whatcha mean?" growled Hardboiled.

The patrolman waved his club. "You just told me to leave the roadster. You were back there somewhere when you called."

"The hell I was!" Hardboiled yelled, and ran for the corner. Sloping around it, he drew up and began to swear.

The roadster was gone.

"You lunk!" Hardboiled accused the policeman. "I told you to watch that machine."

"But you told me to leave it, too," declared the cop.

"I did not!" Hardboiled growled. "Are you calling me a liar?"

"No," said the patrolman prudently. "I must be crazy."

A few blocks distant, Doc Savage tooled the roadster through the late afternoon traffic. He was a man of a myriad accomplishments, this bronze giant. Among other things, he was a skilled voice mimic and ventriloquist. It had been a simple matter to imitate Hardboiled's gruff tone and get the patrolman away from the roadster.

From time to time, the bronze man leaned over and spoke into the radio microphone, calling, "Monk, Ham," but getting no answer.

The apparatus operated on a short wavelength, and, compact though it was, it had power enough to communicate over a number of miles, even through the highly unfavorable conditions set up by the towering buildings of the city.

Doc called again, "Monk, Ham."

The childlike voice of Monk said, "On deck, Doc," from the loudspeaker.

"Did you manage to trail the sniper?" Doc Savage asked.

"Sure," Monk answered. "We've got him spotted. He's in a taxicab going down Broadway."

"Don't lose him," Doc Savage requested.

The bronze man now wheeled the roadster to the right, and shortly afterward was traversing the rich canyon of Park Avenue, passing towering apartment houses which housed more wealthy persons per block than perhaps any other thoroughfare in the world.

Shortly afterward, the roadster pulled up before an elaborately modernistic structure situated in the most exclusive section of the avenue. Two doormen in resplendent uniforms bowed Doc Savage inside and the bronze man entered a reception room where he was met by an exquisitely gowned redheaded young woman who politely inquired his business.

"I want to speak to Pat," Doc said.

The titian receptionist was a beauty, but she was completely overshadowed by the young woman who soon put in an appearance.

This young woman was tall, had an exquisite form, and wore a stunning gown. The striking point about her appearance was her wealth of bronze hair—it was almost the same hue as Doc Savage's hair. She looked very regal in the long, trailing gown.

Several males of varying ages waiting in the large, sumptuously furnished reception room sighed as they saw the bronze-haired vision.

"Hello, Pat," Doc Savage said.

Pat asked, "Well, who's trying to kill you now?"

Pat was Patricia Savage, cousin to the man of bronze, Doc Savage. Pat liked excitement, and had long ago sought to join the unusual group of five assistants with which Doc Savage had surrounded himself.

Doc, considering association with himself too dangerous, had refused to consider it. But the bronze man frequently employed Pat's aid. Between adventures, Pat devoted herself to running this combination beauty parlor and gymnasium which catered to the very rich. Financially, she was very successful.

"Want to help me?" Doc asked her.

"That," laughed Pat, "is equivalent to an invitation to be shot at, stabbed, drowned, beaten up and no telling what else. Sure, I'll help you. Who are we fighting?"

"So far, the whole affair is strange," Doc told her. "A gunman killed Leander Court, then the gunman had a fit and fell over dead with his eyes protruding. The way he died was very mysterious."

"Do you know what caused the pop-eyed death?" Pat asked.

"No," Doc told her promptly.

"Then it *must* be mysterious," Pat murmured. "What am I to do?"

Doc Savage gave a brief synopsis of all that had occurred.

"Janko Sultman's business is running the Association of Physical Health," he finished. "I want you to scout around there and see what you can turn up."

"Any suggestion about how I am to do it?" Pat asked.

"Use your own excellent judgment," Doc told her. "But watch out for a tough cop called Hardboiled Humbolt."

"I've been reading about him in the newspapers," Pat smiled. "The new mayor put him in charge of Manhattan to clean up. They say that this alone was enough to scare half the crooks out of town. He must be a ripsnorter."

"He is all of that," Doc agreed. "He has already placed me under arrest."

"Goodness!" exploded Pat. "What for?"

"He endeavored to bulldoze information out of me," Doc said dryly. "Unluckily, he wanted to know something that could not be divulged."

"What?"

"He tried to learn what connection Leander Court had with myself," Doc Savage said.

Pat's features suddenly became grim. "Listen, Doc, do you think some one could be trying——".

"It's too early to tell," the bronze man said. "And I've got to be moving."

The armored roadster carried the bronze man south quietly and swiftly. He switched on the two-way radio apparatus and Monk's small voice began coming from the speaker, making explanations.

"Me and Ham were in the street when we heard the noise of a silenced rifle and heard the bullet hit the window," Monk stated. "We decided the shot must have come from the roof and we reasoned the gunman would come out in the next block, so we barged around there and sure enough, a lad pops out. He's a thin-looking egg with a face like one of them old Salem witches. He dived into a cab. It's him all right. He's got his guns in the trombone case."

"Where are you now?" the bronze man inquired.

Monk replied with an address far downtown.

Doc Savage angled over to the west side of Manhattan Island, took the elevated express highway which led southward, and eventually came out on Canal Street, where there were numberless trucks, taxicabs and a few horsedrawn drays.

An excited squeak, Monk's small voice jumped out of the radio. "The sniper is gettin' out of his hack!"

"Keep a line on him," Doc requested.

"O.K.," said Monk. "The bird has gone into a department store across the street."

"Sure you can watch all entrances to the store?" Doc asked.

"You bet!" Monk's small voice was confident. "We've got our heap parked close to the corner. The guy must have gone into the store to buy something."

The next few seconds produced no more direct communication, although Doc Savage caught a number of sarcastic exchanges between the small-voiced Monk and his companion, "Ham," who had a well-developed orator's voice. The two seemed to be on the verge of a fight.

Doc Savage ignored the verbal hostilities. Monk and Ham always seemed on the verge of a fight; no one acquainted with the pair could recall one of them having addressed a civil word to the other. They squabbled continuously about anything and everything, and they were actually friends who would sacrifice everything for each other.

The bronze man devoted his attention to working through a fleet of drygoods trucks which were evidently bound for retail centers adjacent to New York City.

Unexpected, explosive, Monk's small voice croaked out of the radio speaker. "Here, you, what's the idea——"

A very brittle and totally strange voice said, "You two mugs have been shaggin' the wrong guy!"

Doc Savage listened intently to the radio speaker, but almost at once, a loud snap of a sound came from it, and after that a shrill oscillating whine, a mournful, hair-raising wail which indicated something had happened to the transmitter in the car occupied by Monk and Ham.

Chapter III

THE BOKE MEETING

The gunman was very lean, with dreamy blue eyes and an extraordinarily long chin which swung down and out to attain the contour which artists like to give to the features of witch drawings. He had used his trombone case to smash in the front of the box which held the transmitting-and-receiving apparatus. His other hand, the left, juggled an automatic pistol which seemed composed mostly of barrel.

Monk rolled one eye at the department store across the street and growled, "How'd you get out of there and come up behind us?"

The witch-faced man held his weapon below the level of the door, where it was out of sight, which was fortunate, because many of the pedestrians who passed turned to stare at the coupé and its occupants. Monk was undoubtedly the magnet which drew their attention.

Monk's physical appearance was startling. Perhaps three out of four citizens who passed were taller than Monk, but Monk weighed in excess of two hundred and fifty pounds, was nearly as tall as he was broad, and had arms some inches longer than his legs. He had a leathery skin, furred with hair that looked like coarse, rusted steel wool. His face was almost incredibly homely, the mouth being far too large.

"Sap!" said the gunman. "That department store has a branch on this side of the street. A tunnel under the street connects the two buildings."

Monk, blinking his small eyes, looked unutterably stupid—which showed how deceptive appearances can be, for Monk, under his full name of Lieutenant Colonel Andrew Blodgett Mayfair, was known as an industrial chemist whose ability was that of a wizard.

The man with the automatic looked at the other occupant of the car—Ham. Major General Theodore Marley Brooks—it was with this name that Ham was formally designated—looked like a gentleman who might qualify as a perfume salesman or a male clerk in an exclusive feminine shop.

He was a wasp-waisted man with the large mobile mouth of an orator and a pair of brightly intent eyes. His garments were sartorial perfection—from creased afternoon trousers to gray derby. He held a thin, plain black cane across his knees.

Ham was also a gentleman who belied his appearance, being one of the most astute lawyers ever to acquire an accent and a degree from Harvard.

The witch-faced gunman, looking puzzled, shook his head slowly but did not divert the menace of his automatic.

"I don't get this," he growled. "Are you two guys laws?"

Ham said in an aggravating, drawling accent, "Really, old fellow, you do misuse the English language dreadfully."

"Horse collar!" said the man with the gun. "Why'd you two tail me."

Ham began, "My dear chap——" Then he stopped and watched the other.

The gunman was wearing a topcoat of some furry gray material, and he stepped back, burying his gun in a pocket of the coat. It was chilly on the street and perfectly natural that a man should keep a hand in a pocket.

"I'll let Boke talk to you," he said. "Let's stagger along."

"Huh?" The homely Monk blinked small eyes.

"Get a move on," advised the other.

"Who's Boke?" Monk demanded.

"We're going for a walk," the man said.

The witch-faced fellow now opened the car door, stepping back with it as if performing a polite service, but he kept his eyes high, watching the faces of Monk and Ham, and their hands. When they got out of the coupé, he fell in behind them and murmured, "Up the street. Boke's joint is close."

They walked several paces, the chill Fall air pulling breath steam out of their nostrils; a few chill particles of snow, more like hail than flakes, crunched out whitely on the sidewalk.

Monk, chin down in his collar as if cold, said three loud words in an absolutely unintelligible dialect.

The gun wielder growled, "Cut it out, whatever you're tryin' to do."

Then the man gave a mad leap and squawled out in agony, and Monk moved with a speed which indicated he had expected the happening and had set himself. He lunged, both big, hairy hands cupping down on the pocket which held the witch-faced man's hand and gun.

Reaching their objective, Monk's paws closed, wrenched. The whole side came out of the man's gray coat. They began to fight over the wad of cloth, hand and gun. The trombone case dropped.

Ham had tucked his black cane under an arm. He snatched at it now, gave the handle a twist and it pulled apart, disclosed that it was a sword cane. At the tip, and for a few inches back, it was coated with a substance which seemed to have a mucilaginous quality.

Ham, manipulating the sword cane with an expert ease, inserted the daubed tip perhaps a half inch under the shoulder skin of their foe. The results were remarkable.

The witch-faced man stared, turned to see what had pricked him, then began to look dazed. His endeavors to use the gun in spite of Monk's restraining clutch, became feeble. Eventually, he seemed to go completely asleep and it was only the support of Monk and Ham which kept him erect.

At that point, there was a series of satisfied grunting sounds at their feet, and for the first time, the two men looked at the animal which had made the conquest possible. This was a pig.

"Not bad, Habeas," the pleasantly ugly Monk grinned.

Habeas Corpus, the pig, was Monk's pet. Habeas was as freakish an example of the porker species as Monk was of the human race. Habeas had the legs of a dog, a thin, gaunt body and a pair of ears which might have doubled for wings.

Monk expended most of his spare time in training Habeas, with the result that the pig had some unique capabilities. Doc Savage and his five men, when wishing to consult each other in a tongue which eavesdroppers could not understand, used the speech of the ancient Mayans, the civilization which once flourished in Central America. Probably not half a dozen men in the civilized world, outside of themselves, could speak and understand the language. Monk had taught Habeas to obey commands given in Mayan.

The shoat, on the floorboards of the coupé, had escaped the witch-faced man's notice, and his attack, directed by Monk in Mayan, had been a surprise.

"We can't stay here," Ham said briskly, and glared at Habeas. Ham treated the pig with no more civility than he did Monk.

The scuffle, brief as it had been, had attracted notice, causing pedestrians to stop and stare, undecided as to what they should do.

"Move on!" Ham commanded sharply.

This did not secure very pronounced results. No policemen were in sight as yet.

"Let's get this guy to the coupé," Monk grunted. "Doc will want to know about this, and he'll want to look up Boke, whoever he is, when he gets here."

The two men started for the coupé, still supporting their unconscious captive. They did not go far.

There was a flurry on the outskirts of the crowd and a man came plunging through, wielding his elbows. He was a scrawny man, unshaven, somewhat shabbily garbed, and he peered at Monk and Ham as if he were very delighted indeed to see them.

"You're cops!" he gulped excitedly. "I know you're cops. Sure! You made a swell pinch when you got this guy."

Monk squinted small eyes at him. Ham opened his orator's

mouth to say something, but the newcomer spouted on without pause.

"Come on," he snapped. "This mug has been up to some funny business. I want to show you what I accidentally saw in his room."

He wheeled off and Monk and Ham, vastly surprised, tramped along after him, the cold snow making gritting noises underfoot and the heels of their unconscious captive dragging along with a series of raspings. The stranger had picked up the trombone case.

They came to a doorway and the guide muttered, "It's in here. I was waitin' for 'im to come back when I saw you put the hand on 'im."

Monk stopped suddenly. "You were waiting here?" He pointed at the door.

"Yes," said the unkempt man.

Monk pointed at the snow particles which did not lie on the sidewalk in sufficient depth to hold footsteps but which had drifted into the doorway in a shallow, cold bank that was unbroken by tracks or other marks which certainly would have been made by the door opening.

"You're a liar!" Monk said. "A poor one, too."

The shabby stranger coughed as if he were cold, and under cover of the convulsion, his hands made a bewilderingly swift gesture and were suddenly holding a pistol.

"I'm good enough to get by," he said.

The crowd, as curious persons will, had followed the little cavalcade, wondering what it was all about and possessed of a morbid desire to see what would happen. They had not followed quite fast enough, however, for any one to be near enough to catch exactly what passed between Monk, Ham and the stranger.

Three men, burly fellows swathed in mufflers, now detached themselves from the crowd and turned upon it, hardfaced and belligerent of manner.

"Here, beat it!" one of them said, and his words threw small puffs of steam into the frosty air. "G'wan! You don't live here. We're cops."

The crowd melted, sheeplike, as city crowds will do in the face of authority.

Monk said something in the strange, not unmusical Mayan dialect, and the pig, Habeas Corpus, spun and raced down the street, feet making clickings and scratchings.

The man with the gun growled, "You say another word I can't understand and it'll be just too damn bad!"

The men who had turned the crowd back now joined the fellow with the gun and they themselves produced weapons.

"Inside," one said. "You know by now that we saw you playing games with our pal here and come down to invite you in where it's warm." He picked up the trombone case.

Some one laughed, and snow rasped as Monk and Ham mounted, still carrying the man who had been made unconscious by Ham's sword cane. In the door, they looked at each other, then let their burden fall heavily.

"Pick 'im up," they were ordered.

They complied with the command and marched into a passage which seemed colder than the street outside. While guns menaced them, hands searched them. The casual thoroughness of the search showed that these men knew the spots where weapons were carried.

Monk and Ham each wore in an expertly padded holster a firearm which resembled an oversized automatic pistol. These had curled magazines, intricate mechanisms, fine workmanship.

"Damn me," one man said softly. "First rods I ever saw like these."

Another man looked at the guns.

"Hell's bells!" His face blanched; his hands shook a little.

The others eyed him, and one demanded, "Why the chalk and shiver?"

The excited man tapped one weapon. "Doc Savage," he said.

"Listen," some one rapped. "What's this?"

"I've read about these. Only Doc Savage's men carry them. They're supermachine pistols. The bronze guy himself invented them."

There was nothing more said for some seconds. One man took out a cigarette, put it between his lips, then took it away from his mouth and mashed it up between slow-moving fingers. Another man, breathing heavily, went back to the door, and looked out.

"Let's go talk to Boke," some one rapped. "I don't like the way this damned thing is shaping up."

The witch-faced man, reviving from the stupefying effects of the chemical on the end of Ham's sword cane, began to squirm and moan. Ham and Monk stood him on his feet, but his legs refused to support him and bowed, letting him down face-first to the floor. Saliva came from his mouth and puddled on the grimy, cold carpet.

Monk kicked him; the impact rolled the man half over.

"Cut it!" snarled one of the others.

The witch-faced man reached back and rubbed the spot where he had been kicked, then rolled over and jacked himself up by the strength of his arms. Slowly he raised himself erect.

"The kick was what he needed," Monk said gloomily.

One of the men scowled at Monk, then at Ham, and said, "Walk ahead of us—and be sure you got a will all made out before you squawk or make a jump."

The man with the face of a harridan weaved toward the back door, saying, "I've got plenty to tell Boke."

The hallway gave into a cement-floored courtyard which smelled of cold garbage. A cat, the sole living thing in sight, hackled its back and slunk among garbage cans.

Crossing the court, the cavalcade entered a hallway where the air was too hot and mounted stairs, and opened a door. Warm, tobacco-laden air gushed out. A fireplace made fitful red light in the room beyond. The place was windowless. It whitened up blindingly when some one thumbed an electric switch.

Monk and Ham were forced to stand with their faces jammed in corners, not unlike schoolboys receiving punishment. They were warned not to turn around; and Monk, disobeying, was knocked rubber-kneed with a slender stick of stovewood from the fuel rack beside the fireplace.

Some one said, "I wonder what happened to that hog?"

"Hell with the hog!" another snorted. "Hey, Boke, things have been happening!"

One of the most pleasant voices Monk and Ham had ever heard said, "That is to be regretted."

Monk and Ham both turned their heads. The speaker was not in the room. Just where the voice was coming from, they could not tell, for the menace of a clubbing forced them to face into the corners again.

The spokesman began, "We were all watching the back way just in case something might turn up, and we saw——"

"Let Frightful tell it," directed the mysterious, amiable voice.

Monk snorted loudly, suddenly realizing that "Frightful" was the nickname of the witch-faced man.

Frightful, listlessness in his voice showing the effects of the drug on the sword cane, said, "I followed your orders, Boke."

Boke's voice asked pleasantly, "What do you mean?"

"I plugged Janko Sultman in the head," said Frightful.

"You cold-blooded devil!" exploded the pleasant-voiced Boke. "Don't be so definite about such a hideous thing. It gets on my nerves."

The witch-faced Frightful seemed accustomed to this squeamishness on the part of his chief, for he went on rapidly:

"I wanta tell you about a strange thing I saw when I posted myself on the roof," he said. "I could see into Janko Sultman's office, but Sultman wasn't there. The office was empty. But after while a guy come in. Who d'you think it was?"

Instead of answering as expected, Boke's remarkably suave voice said hollowly, "I would give my right arm if it had not been necessary to eliminate Sultman. A murder! Horrible!"

Frightful said, "Leander Court came into Sultman's office while I was watching."

Boke's voice, yelling suddenly, demanded, *"Who?"*

"Leander Court," Frightful repeated patiently. "He sat around in the office by himself until the telephone rang, and he answered it. What he heard must have made him excited. He threw the phone down and broke the glass out of the office door and crawled through. The door must have had a trick lock."

"It has," said pleasant-voiced Boke. "Then what happened?"

"Some guy in the reception room up and fills Leander Court full of bullets. I could see that. Then the guy ran for the stairs. After that, something must've happened to the guy, because I heard some bellowing and a lot of cops came, and I heard one of 'em say something about the guy being dead with his eyes sticking out."

"With what?" demanded Boke.

"His eyes sticking out. Like you've been reading about in the papers."

"It is all very clear to me except that last," said Boke, puzzlement in his amiable tone. "Janko Sultman had double-crossed us, as we already knew, and had an appointment with Leander Court. He must have put his proposition up to Court over the telephone, or perhaps he had already advanced his proposal and Court had come to give his answer.

"Court refused and tried to flee, and the gunman was one who had been posted by Janko Sultman to kill Court in case the latter was stubborn or threatened to go to Doc Savage. Yes. All is very clear. But what happened to the gunman? Are you sure that his eyes popped out?"

"I'm only tellin' you what I overheard," Frightful grumbled.

"Baffling," said Boke. "I cannot understand it."

Monk turned his head in another effort to learn where the voice of Boke was coming from, and one of the guards slugged the homely chemist, knocking him against the wall. Monk lashed back with an astounding speed and the assailant staggered away, his jaw possessed of a slightly different shape than it had had a moment before. Pistol muzzles forced Monk back into his corner and made him face the wall.

"Where did these two men come from?" asked Boke's mysterious voice.

"They got on my trail somehow," snarled Frightful. "They're two of Doc Savage's men."

"They're who?" Boke sounded as if he had swallowed something painful.

"Doc Savage's men," Frightful repeated, then looked very uneasy, and the others registered concern also.

When Boke's unique tone sounded again, worry had gone from it, and he laughed.

"It was only a matter of days, anyway," he said. "Or perhaps of hours. We would have had to fight Doc Savage eventually over this affair. You all know that."

Frightful made a wry face. "I haven't been looking forward to it."

"Hold these two prisoners," Boke ordered. "Then get hold of Leander Court's partner. You know who I mean?"

"Yeah." Frightful nodded. "Robert Lorrey."

"Exactly," said Boke. "Arrange an appointment for me with Robert Lorrey. We must whip things up before Doc Savage gets a line on what it is all about. And do not make the mistake of underrating this man Savage. He is assuredly clever."

A man began, "Don't worry, chief, I don't think any of this crowd underrates that bronze——" He did not finish and his eyes flew roundly open and his jaw sagged enough to pull his lips apart so that his teeth showed. They were not nice teeth, being veined up and down and stained so that they resembled chips from an old bone which had lain a long time in the weather.

The man reached up and felt of his ears as if he suspected them of tricks.

For there was a strange trilling loose in the room.

Chapter IV

MORE POP-EYED

The trilling sound, low and fantastic, was quite musical, yet it was so without adhering to any definite tune. Nor could the exact nature of the sound, the sonic embodiment of the thing itself, be described. It was something that defied nomenclature, something infinitely etheric, yet also very real, for it was at times quite loud, and again it sank into virtual inaudibility.

Monk and Ham turned slowly in the corners, eyes alert, muscles tensing. They knew this weird trilling. It was the sound of Doc Savage, a small and unconscious thing which the giant of bronze did in moments of stress.

"Hey!" Monk howled suddenly and pointed at the ceiling. "Look! For cryin' out loud!"

Almost all eyes went to the ceiling. Monk was an actor when he wanted to be. But two or three were not misled by the ruse, and it was they who saw the door snap open to let in a Herculean metal figure who, in passing through, all but filled the aperture.

"Talk about the devil——" a man roared, and raced a hand for his gun pocket.

Doc Savage came toward him with the speed of light spurted from a bronze-tinted lens—and stopped. He stood frozen. Then he began to back away.

Monk and Ham stared, puzzled, not comprehending why the bronze man had hesitated, nor able to remember a time when he had done so in the past.

The man got his gun out, weaved a bit on his feet as if his leg muscles were unsteady, and took aim.

Only then did Doc Savage flash in. But it seemed too late. The gun was a revolver, and the trigger finger was already tightening.

The way Doc Savage, giant of metal, reached the gunman and seized the weapon was something Monk and Ham always remembered. They had seen the bronze giant move swiftly before, but never with quite this unearthly speed. And when the man of bronze stepped back, they saw why he had at first hesitated to attack the would-be killer.

The man's eyes were popping. When he had lost his gun,

the man staggered a pace after Doc Savage, then brought up and swung a hand foolishly against his own face. He felt of his own eyes, almost out of their sockets, in a manner that was hideous to watch, for it was apparent that the fellow could no longer see.

Then he began to shriek and bend and unbend himself in convulsions of frightful agony; he fell upon the floor, spread himself out and his clenched fists beat the rough carpet until the skin was barked off.

Then another man began to shriek, to paw at his face, to flail his arms as if fighting an unseen, hideous harpy.

A third joined the unearthly chorus, and a fourth, then others, until the room was a bedlam with bodies threshing about and shrieks that split the ears.

A man fell headlong into the fireplace, and the flames consumed his hair with a malodorous *swoosh!* and his flesh began to sizzle while he screeched as if trying to empty himself of all that nature had put within him.

Monk ran over, seized upon the man's heels and dragged him out, still howling. The only cooling agent at hand seemed to be a bottle of pale amber wine, and Monk poured that upon the victim; but the fellow continued to thresh, dying within a few moments.

Monk backed away, horror on his homely face. Monk was hard; men had tried to kill him, and he had seen hideous things happen to human bodies. But now his nerves became as old strings; cold water seemed to wash through his veins and his big mouth felt tongueless.

He realized, almost suddenly, that it was quiet in the room of fantastic death, with bodies twisted horrors on the floor and with only Doc Savage, Ham and himself erect.

Monk tried three times before he could speak.

"What in blazes happened?" he mumbled.

When Monk got no answer, he looked at Doc Savage, after which his own feeling of amazement increased a bit, if such were possible, for there was stark bewilderment on Doc Savage's regular, metallic features. And Doc Savage rarely showed emotion.

"You—don't know—what it was?" Monk asked haltingly.

The bronze man shook a slow negative. "I only know that it was one of the most hideous, mysterious things I have ever seen happen."

"Every one of them died but us—every one in the room but us," Ham said, and looked steadily at the ceiling as if to avoid the bodies on the floor. "How do you explain that?"

Monk, stepping high over corpses, announced, "I'm gettin' out of here. The damn *thing* that killed 'em may have another try—at us."

Doc Savage shook his head again, half in negations, half in puzzlement.

"If it had been gas, it would have killed us," he said. "There was no sound, no firing of hidden darts, and if they had been poisoned—— Impossible! No poison would have affected them all at once."

"A death ray of some kind, maybe," Ham muttered.

"You dope," Monk told him unkindly. "A death ray would have gotten us, too."

Doc Savage rapped, "Just before I came, another man was talking, a man they addressed as Boke. Where was he?"

Monk waved his arms. "Danged if I know. That was queer, too. His voice was plain, but he wasn't in here."

"This Boke, he was their chief?" Doc asked.

Ham answered that. "Righto. And the beggar seemed to think he had been double-crossed by Janko Sultman. He ordered Sultman shot." Ham eyed the contorted body of Frightful, the witch-faced one, who reposed at his feet, quite dead.

"I heard most of it," Doc Savage said. "The pig, Habeas Corpus, was down in the street when I got there, and it was easy to tell from the tracks what had happened. I came in right behind you, it would seem."

"Where's Habeas now?" Monk demanded.

"Downstairs," Doc advised.

Ham waved his sword cane, which he had retrieved from where one of their late unfortunate captors had placed it.

"But what killed these men?" he demanded.

Doc Savage hazarded slowly, "The same thing which killed the murderer of Leander Court; I think we can be assured of that."

"But what was it?" Ham persisted.

"Believe me, I was never before so much at a loss for an explanation of a happening," Doc Savage said quietly.

"Which makes it a real mystery," Monk grumbled.

"We will look around," Doc Savage said. "We may find something that will help."

They began to search.

Ham, as if he had thought of something, interjected, "You heard this mysterious Boke say he was going to talk to Robert Lorrey?"

"Yes," Doc agreed. "We will look into that, also."

Monk growled, "Do you reckon this has got something to do with our upstate——"

"Some one might be listening," Doc said sharply.

Monk fell silent, for there was one subject which Doc Savage and his men did not discuss publicly. That was the matter of their unique "college" in the remote wooded mountains of upstate New York.

As far as they knew, none beyond those immediately concerned knew of that "college," those concerned being Doc Savage, his five aides, Pat Savage, and the attendants in the institution itself. The students who enrolled in that college and, later, were graduated, did not even know its whereabouts.

For the students entered unwillingly, usually under the affects of a stupor-inducing drug. When they left after graduation, they were also drugged.

The students were criminals, and the "college" was a fantastic place which turned them into honest men whether they wished it or not. The world did not know about the place. The world would probably have been shocked.

In charge of the criminal-curing institution was a man named Robert Lorrey, a scientific surgeon of fabulous skill whom Doc Savage himself had trained.

What Robert Lorrey did to the criminals that made them honest men was known only to himself and to his chief assistant at the institution—or rather, the man who had been his chief assistant—Leander Court, the man shot down in cold blood in the reception room of the Association of Physical Health. What he did had to do with intricate surgery, chemical rehabilitation, and there was also a long course of training. Doc Savage, of course, knew.

When criminals emerged from Doc Savage's unique university, they did not remember their pasts; for some strange reason they hated crime in any form, and they had been taught a trade wherewith to make an honest living.

Had the existence of this place become known, it would have been a newspaper story unparalleled. Doc Savage also knew it would excite many misguided reformers who would stir up government investigations, for the criminals had no choice about taking the treatment.

Doc Savage, in the final analysis, was a private individual, and such are not supposed to mete out their own brand of justice. The courts are for that. And Doc Savage had never sent a crook before an American court.

If news of his "college" got out, there would be all kinds

of trouble, he well knew, and for that reason he had refused to tell the two-fisted tough guy cop, Hardboiled Humbolt, of murdered Leander Court's connection with himself.

And it was to keep news of the institution from leaking out that the bronze man now requested Monk not to speak of it. What Monk was wondering was perfectly plain anyway. Was the "college" in some way connected with this fantastic affair?

Monk growled, "What I want to know is where that guy Boke was. He wasn't in this room. I'll swear to that. I dang near got my head caved in lookin' for 'im."

Ham said unkindly, "No such luck," and added, "What do you say we try some of the other rooms?"

They tried some of the other rooms—all of them in fact, and found them an unsavory collection of dungeons, unfurnished for the most part, with those that were equipped fitted up with shoddy stuff.

"Looks kinda like a temporary hangout," Monk decided.

They had found no one, no sign of the nebulous Boke, the man with the voice that was so utterly pleasant.

The rendezvous had, they discovered, a galaxy of entrances. Several buildings on both sides of the cheap block had been rented, it seemed, and connecting doors cut through them.

They went through the whole maze, the process requiring the better part of an hour, but found no sign of Boke. Doc Savage himself searched the roof, which was cold and bare, being without a coping so that the chill wind whooped across it without interruption.

Doc Savage stood for a time on the roof, apparently unaffected by the cold, close to where the smoke poured from a chimney that led to the fireplace in the death room below. Then he went down to the macabre chamber itself.

The bronze man began sounding the walls. The room, it was plain, had once been much longer, but had been shut off by two partitions. These were thin, and constructed of a wallboard with a paper exterior.

A moment later his fist, in pumping against the panels, went through.

"Blazes!" Monk snorted. "There is where the guy was speaking from! He was in the next room, and that paper was what made his voice sound a little queer."

"I did notice that his voice was muffled," Ham admitted. "But it was such a pleasant voice that the muffled quality almost escaped my attention."

"That," Monk said, "explains part of the mystery."

Doc Savage moved toward the door.

"We had better go talk to Robert Lorrey," he declared. "He is at the—where he works—and we can get him by short-wave radio telephone. As for Boke, he must have been unaffected by whatever killed those men. He made his getaway during the excitement."

"Have you any idea what caused the deaths?" Monk asked bluntly.

Doc Savage seemed to become inexplicably deaf and not to hear, a fact which caused Monk to grin widely, because he knew from past events that it was a good sign when Doc began keeping his own counsel.

Doc rarely expressed a theory which he could not prove absolutely, but if he had no theory and was completely mystified, he would say so. Hence Doc's assumed deafness conveyed to Monk that the bronze man did have an idea about the strange Boke.

Going downstairs, they found Habeas Corpus there, shivering. It was near dusk, with the streets almost deserted.

The uproar in the house as the men died so weirdly and so awfully, apparently had not carried to the street, thanks in part to the first gale of Fall, which had whipped itself up to quite a frenzy, driving the hard snow with the force of cold bullets.

The bronze man drove his open roadster, seeming not to feel the cold. Monk and Ham followed in their coupé, the windows up, the heater on to its fullest. They had resumed their interminable quarrel, the present point of dissent being Monk's driving.

They headed directly for the middle of Central Park, the most open space that the metropolis offered, where conditions were best for radio transmission and reception. Doc Savage tuned in and called over the short-wave set, and Monk and Ham tuned in on their apparatus, listening.

Eventually, Doc got the upstate "college."

"Robert Lorrey," he requested.

"Who!" The distant voice, that of an attendant at the institution, seemed surprised. "Two days ago, you telegraphed Robert Lorrey to take his vacation."

"*I* telegraphed him?" Doc Savage asked slowly.

"Why, yes—at least the message had your name signed to it," said the distant voice. "Robert Lorrey left this morning."

"Did he say where he was going to spend his vacation?" the bronze man demanded.

"No," said the attendant. "Your message told him not to communicate with you, so that he would have a completely uninterrupted rest."

Doc Savage's lips did not move, but there was not silence in the roadster, for the bronze man's fantastic trilling sound came into being, persisted a moment, then ebbed away.

"And what about Leander Court?" Doc asked.

"Why, a telegram from you gave him his vacation four days earlier," advised the attendant. "I trust there is nothing wrong."

Doc Savage countered with another question. "Is everything all right around there?"

"Yes, of course."

"Double the guards," the bronze man directed. "Go over the electrical alarm system and the sonic amplifier listening posts to see that they have not been tampered with."

"Yes, sir," agreed the attendant. "Then something *is* wrong?"

"I am afraid so," Doc told him.

"What is it?"

"That is impossible to say, as yet."

This terminated the radio-telephonic hookup.

Monk and Ham got out of their coupé, shivered in the chill air and came over.

"You heard it?" Doc asked them.

Ham nodded soberly and ran his sword cane through gloved fingers.

"Did you telegraph a vacation to either Leander Court or Robert Lorrey?" he asked.

"No," Doc Savage said.

As Doc Savage drove out of the park and downtown, he and his companions could not help but note the attitude with which the stories of the pop-eyed deaths were being received by the public.

Newsboys ran along the streets, screaming headlines concerning the passing of Leander Court, and they did a surprising business. Housewives ran out to purchase papers. Groups of persons stood in front of cigar stores and under street lamps, in spite of the cold.

In pausing for a traffic light, they could hear a man speaking in a near-by car.

"It's something like the influenza epidemic, only worse," he was saying. "I tell you, I'm right! Mark my words. In a few days, there'll be thousands dying! Women, kids and men—they'll all die. I know what I'm talking about."

"I've already sent my family out of town," said another man in the car.

"I'm taking a train to-night," said the other. "It's the only thing to do. I know what I'm talking about, I tell you. These poor devils who stay behind may catch that damned disease that kills you with your eyes sticking out. It's a risk, too much of a risk for me. I can see what's coming."

Driving onward, Doc Savage stopped at his headquarters on the eighty-sixth floor of a skyscraper which was one of the most impressive in the city.

The bronze man's establishment there consisted of an outer office, plainly and expensively furnished, a library containing one of the most complete assortments of scientific volumes in existence, and a laboratory fitted with every modern device, as well as a great amount of apparatus which was the bronze man's own invention.

"What next?" Monk wanted to know, he and Ham having followed Doc.

"Renny," Doc replied. "He is in town and will want in on this. He was consulting on an engineering job this afternoon, and I failed to locate him when the call came about Leander Court."

Monk nodded, comprehending.

"Renny"—Colonel John Renwick—was another member of Doc Savage's group of five unusual aides. Renny was noted for two things: his tremendous fists, and his ability as an engineer.

He had a face peculiar for the expression it wore. Renny always looked as if he were going to the funeral of a very close friend. Renny also had two loves: he liked excitement, and it was his boast that he could smash the panel out of the strongest wooden door built with a single blow of his incredible fists.

Doc Savage made several telephone calls, but was unable to locate the big-fisted Renny.

The bronze man then went to the large office window and with a bit of peculiar looking substance, wrote rapidly on the glass. Nothing appeared after he had written. The unusual chalk he had employed left a mark which could not be seen except with the aid of an ultra-violet lantern. Under these invisible rays the stuff would fluoresce, or glow, appearing in an eerie electric blue.

Renny, when he reached the headquarters, would use an ultra-violet projector, a small one which reposed in the desk, to examine the window. It was Doc's custom to leave messages thus.

Two other members of Doc Savage's group of five were not at present in New York. "Long Tom" Roberts, the electrical wizard, was in Chicago, attending an exposition of electrical inventions in which he had exhibits. "Johnny"—William Harper Littlejohn—archæologist and geologist, was filling the chair of natural science research at a famous university during the illness of a professor who regularly occupied that position.

"Now what?" persisted Monk. Then he suddenly slapped a hand on his knee, a feat which he could accomplish without bending in the slightest. "Say, I just thought of a way that we can maybe locate Robert Lorrey!"

"Through his brother, Sidney?" Doc queried.

Monk looked crestfallen. "So you thought of that."

"Yes," said Doc. "We'll try Sidney Lorrey now."

Chapter V

THE HAND OF SULTMAN

Robert and Sidney Lorrey were twin brothers, and, twinlike, had the same interests and dislikes, and it was not strange that they should both have become scientists.

Robert had long ago associated himself with Doc Savage in a position which paid him more money, perhaps, than he could have made at any other profession. The other twin, Sidney, had a laboratory in New York City and spent his time there experimenting and inventing.

Both brothers were graduate surgeons and doctors. Robert practiced what he knew. Sidney, on the other hand, was the creative member of the pair. His prize invention was an apparatus which produced the same emanations as radium, without radium's terrific expense, although he did not yet have this device refined where it could be used as a commercial proposition. He believed his device would be an inestimable boon in treating cancer and other diseases.

Sidney Lorrey's laboratory was on a barge which was moored to a long-disused pier in the East River.

Doc Savage's party, approaching the barge, inspected it closely for lights. The craft was long, shabby-looking, blunt at the ends; and in the middle, where the cargo pit would ordinarily have been, there was a long, neat, white deck house. Nowhere did a light show. They could hear the low whine of electrical apparatus.

The three men paused to study the craft, and because it was cold, Habeas Corpus, the pig, planted himself against Ham's neatly pressed trousers to get the benefit of whatever warmth there was in the dapper lawyer's ankles.

Ham struck fiercely at the shoat with his sword cane. The pig, accustomed to such moves, got clear.

"One of these days I shall make breakfast bacon out of that hog!" Ham promised grimly.

"You try it and there'll just be a grease spot where you stood!" Monk told him with equal grimness.

They advanced and observed that the tide was going out noisily, causing a grinding of fenders and a creaking of hawsers. Upstream, as the tide ran now, a low log of a boat was anchored, the smell coming from it indicating it to be a gasoline barge.

Doc Savage led the way aboard Sidney Lorrey's barge, glanced about and rapped on the door. The panel was of steel and his knuckles drummed hollowly against it.

There was no answer. They went to the windows, found them barred heavily, and threw flashlights inside. The whine was louder.

"Probably has to keep things fastened up on account of sneak thieves," Monk hazarded. "That whine must be one of his devices."

The probing flashlight beams picked up chemical paraphernalia inside the barge laboratory, together with the coils and tubes of electrical devices, as well as tools and workbenches.

"Bally lot of equipment he has," Ham remarked.

"No one home, obviously," Doc Savage said. "We will leave a note on the door, and try to telephone him later."

The bronze man wrote briefly on a bit of paper and was wedging it in a crack of the barge door with a match stick when Monk barked, "Hey! Lookit!"

Upstream, a man had appeared. He seemed to be in an intoxicated condition, for he weaved along the bulkhead, stumbling and staggering. Reaching the edge, he leaned over groggily and peered at the water below.

"Get back, you numbskull!" Monk bellowed, small voice suddenly tremendous. "You'll fall in!"

The man looked up at the sound of Monk's voice. The effort seemed to overbalance him. His arms cart-wheeled and he toppled into the cold, black race below.

"Blast it!" Monk gritted. "Of all nights to have to jump into the river after some lug!"

He started for the water, wrenching long arms out of his coat. Then Doc Savage's flashlight beam dived past him, roved the water briefly, and the bronze man's forceful clutch fell on his shoulder.

"Don't dive in," Doc warned.

Monk gulped, "But that fool will drown!"

"Take a look at the water," Doc advised.

Monk peered down.

"For the love of mud!" he muttered.

The water, where the flashlight beam fell upon, gave back all the colors of the rainbow in a convulsing, eerie fashion. It was as if pigment of many colors had been spilled on the boiling surface of the tide rip.

"Gasoline," Doc Savage said shortly. "That fellow must have opened a dump valve in the gas boat over there."

Monk yelled, "A trap!"

And Ham echoed, "He thought some of us would jump in and swim toward him, then somebody would set fire to the gasoline on top of the water."

Doc Savage whipped for the heavy gangplank that led from the barge to the shore.

Down in the water, the splashing man suddenly shed his clumsiness. He stroked furiously, reached the bulkhead and grabbed a rope which was almost indistinguishable in the darkness but which he must have lowered previously. He climbed with frenzied haste.

Nearing the top, the fellow snaked a hand into his coat for a gun, then kept one finger hooked through the trigger guard as he continued to climb. He kept his face upturned.

A head, its bronze color discernible even in the gloom, appeared above. The man on the rope reversed his gun swiftly and fired. He saw the bronze head plainly the instant before the lash of flame from the gun muzzle blotted it out. Afterward, the head was gone.

Confident he had killed the bronze man, the fellow on the rope jerked himself up to the bulkhead edge, elbowed over, and looked for his victim. He swore. There was no one distinguishable.

Amazement held the would-be killer for a moment. He was positive his bullet had not missed; he did not believe any one could have gotten out of the path of the slug so swiftly.

Grunting with the effort, he hauled himself up on the

bulkhead, took a tentative pace away from the river, his gun ready.

Off to the left, there was a single firecracker pop of a noise. The man with the gun cursed, hopped on one leg, then tried to run, but negotiated only a few paces before he floundered down. His legs still beat the ground after he lay prone, as if he were trying to continue running.

Monk got up from behind an old timber, waving his supermachine pistol which he had taken from his former captives in the strange room of death downtown.

"You got an antidote for the chemical in the mercy bullets these guns shoot?" he demanded of Doc Savage.

"In the car," the bronze man said, and glided for his roadster.

Doc Savage came back shortly with a hypodermic needle, the contents of which he administered to the victim.

Monk stood expectantly in the background. The supermachine pistols were charged, not with regulation bullets, but with shells which bore a chemical that produced a harmless unconsciousness, and the stuff Doc was giving the victim was a stimulant which would revive him quickly.

The manner of the would-be killer's reviving was a bit queer. His legs had gradually ceased to make their running movements, but now they resumed, and the churning became more violent, until the fellow grunted loudly, opened his eyes and tried to get up.

Monk turned him over and sat on the pit of his stomach.

"You're in a spot, sonny," Monk advised him.

The "sonny" was sarcasm, for the man was past middle age. He had, however, a face of consummate evil. His mouth was warped from a perpetual snarl and his eyes were narrow, furtive.

The man growled thickly, "Aw, I just fell in——"

"You cannot lie out of it," Doc Savage told him. "But you can help your own position by talking."

The evil-faced man scowled at the bronze giant, then looked away and his face convulsed as he wet his lips.

"I dunno nothin'," he disclaimed.

Monk, saying nothing, reached out a hairy arm to a pile of rusted scrap iron which lay on the bulkhead. He selected a heavy gear wheel, pulled it to him, wrenched off the victim's belt and began strapping the weight to the fellow's ankle.

"Cut it out," gritted the other. "You can't do that."

"You know who we are?" Monk asked him.

The other wet his lips once more. "Sure. Doc Savage and two of his gang."

"Ever hear what happens to crooks who get in our way?" Monk demanded fiercely.

The old man snarled, "You ain't runnin' no shandy on me!"

"Listen," Monk said patiently. "I asked you if you ever heard what happens to crooks who tangle up with us."

"No." The captive tried to kick the heavy gear off his ankle.

"They disappear," Monk leered. "They ain't never heard from again. That's what happens to guys who mix with us. You've heard that story, ain't you?"

The terrified roll of the prisoner's eyes showed that he had heard of the legend that those who opposed Doc Savage met some fantastic fate, and were never seen again by their former associates. This was the story the underworld bandied, for none knew of Doc Savage's strange "college" for curing criminals.

"You're another one that's not gonna be heard from," said Monk.

The homely chemist was bluffing, but nothing on his simian features revealed that.

The captive broke suddenly.

"Listen!" he exploded. "I hada do it. I needed the money. I'm an old man and things are tough for me. I got a bad record and nobody'll give me work."

"Who hired you?" Doc Savage asked sharply.

Monk began untying the heavy flywheel to encourage their source of information.

"A guy named Sultman—Janko Sultman," gulped the elderly thug.

"Blazes!" said Monk. "Are you sure it wasn't a bird with a nice voice named Boke?"

"Sultman was his name," the other insisted. "He told me to watch this barge here and if you birds showed up, to pull that falling-into-the-river gag. I was gonna——" He hesitated, and then stopped speaking.

"I know," Monk told him sourly. "You was gonna set the gasoline afire after one of us jumped in. What is Sultman's game?"

"I don't know," insisted the old man. "He didn't spill that part. He come here lookin' for Robert Lorrey, but there wasn't nobody on the barge and he left me here to tell 'im if Robert Lorrey came back, an' to—well—if you guys showed up."

"You know no more than that?" Doc Savage asked.

"That's all."

Monk said fiercely, "Cough up the truth, mug, or I'll bust you wide open!"

The old crook began cursing.

A harsh voice said, "All right, you clever boys will all put your hands up!"

Ham drifted a hand for the armpit where reposed his super-machine pistol laden with mercy bullets.

"Careful," Doc warned. "It's our friend Hardboiled Humbolt."

Hardboiled came out of the shadows, a belligerent tower of gristle who walked gingerly, favoring his sore feet. His hands were empty.

Behind him strode uniformed policemen who carried submachine guns, riot shotguns and tear gas paraphernalia.

Hardboiled leveled an arm at Doc Savage. "I put you under arrest once to-day. What's the idea? Think I was kidding you?"

Monk said mildly, "Tough guys are my meat!" and got off the aged criminal. He went toward Hardboiled Humbolt, and when he was very close to the giant officer, things happened. Monk lashed out a fist that landed with a sound akin to a woodsman's axe sinking into a tree.

Monk looked confident that Hardboiled would go down. But nothing of the sort happened. Hardboiled did tremble and weave on his feet, then his arm shook and the blackjack came down out of his sleeve. There was a swishing sound; Monk ducked, but not in time.

The homely chemist sat down heavily, wearing a dazed expression and feeling of the top of his head where the sap had landed.

Ham laughed unkindly.

Habeas Corpus made a staccato grunting outburst and ran at Hardboiled Humbolt. The policeman kicked at the shoat, but he must have been half-unconscious from the effects of Monk's blow, because he lost his balance and fell heavily. The pig rushed him again, showing long yellow tusks.

Monk said horsely, "Cut it out, Habeas. That guy is really hard," and the pig backed away again.

The elderly crook got up and tried to run. A policeman tripped him and put a foot on the back of his neck, not at all gently.

"I know this old punk," said the cop. "He's a rat from way back."

Hardboiled Humbolt, still sitting on the cold ground, waved his blackjack at Doc Savage, at Monk, at Ham.

"Run 'em in!" he directed. "I warned this bronze guy!"

Ham, the lawyer, drew himself up and snapped, "My rough-mannered friend, men are not arrested in these good United States unless——"

"There is a charge against 'em!" Hardboiled finished for him. "And you can bet your pretty striped pants that there is a charge against all three of you. It is suspicion of murder."

Ham said, "Ridiculous!" as if it were a swear word.

Hardboiled Humbolt, reciting as if he were in school, said, "Over half a dozen men were found a short time ago, dead in a downtown house. Their eyes were all protruding. Witnesses were found who saw you three men leave the house."

A scowl wrinkled high on Ham's forehead. "Better not start anything you can't finish, Mister Tough Policeman."

"We got a call," Hardboiled elaborated. "It said to go to this house and we would find a crowd of men you had murdered."

Doc Savage put into the conversation for the first time with the demand, "Who was the informant?"

"Didn't give his name," said Hardboiled. "But it was a damned pleasant voice to listen to."

"Boke," Monk growled.

"What?" demanded Hardboiled.

"Fooey on you," Monk told him.

The elderly thug on the ground, with the cop's foot on his neck, abruptly seized the policeman's other foot with his hands and yanked, spilling the officer.

The lawman swore and the submachine gun he was carrying bounced out of his hands. The aged criminal seized it.

Startled policemen tried to get their weapons into action, but they were too late and they stared, aghast, as the machine gun fanned them menacingly.

The ancient crook started to back away, escape his main thought. Then another idea seemed to seize him and he paused, stepped sidewise and was sheltered behind a rusting lump of abandoned machinery.

"Damn you all!" he gritted. "I've always wanted to slough me a bunch of cops!" He braced the submachine gun more firmly.

"I told you he was a rat," choked one of the policemen. "He's a crazy killer!"

They all expected the rapid-firer to blare out; but instead, it was the old man's voice which tore a guttural shriek, and he came staggering and moaning from the shelter. He had dropped his gun.

His eyes were popping in a fashion ghastly to observe.

To Doc Savage, Monk and Ham, who had seen what happened in the death room downtown, what occurred now was not new. But to the policeman, it was a sight they were to carry always.

The old criminal was a victim of the pop-eyed death, and he shrieked and bit his lips until they ran scarlet; then he fell down with convulsions and finally kicked his life away.

Hardboiled Humbolt squirmed his feet in his oversize sneakers and wet his lips; his hands made the small aimless gestures of a man who does not know what to do, and he breathed heavily. He was the picture of a phlegmatic soul startled out of his wits.

The homely Monk, getting slowly to his feet, a hand still up where Hardboiled's blackjack had landed, moved close to Doc.

"We gonna let this cop throw us into the can?" he demanded in a whisper.

Hardboiled Humbolt snapped off his lethargy, came over and clipped, "No talking between you three!"

Monk glared at him and demanded, "You mean we're really pinched?"

"And how!" the burly officer said with gusto. "For once, some of you privileged boys in this town are going to take what's coming to you."

Ham asked, "Did you stop to think?"

"Think what?" Hardboiled looked puzzled.

"That Doc Savage, here, may not be in the same class with the rest of these people you call 'privileged'," Ham elaborated. "The persons you are down on are those with so-called 'pull,' politicians and playboys and so on. Now Doc, here——"

"Is going to jail," Hardboiled finished. "I don't give a damn if he's the governor of the state in disguise. And you, you fashion-plate lawyer, are going along."

"It's an outrage," said Ham.

"It's murder!" Hardboiled waved at the dead man. "Damned mysterious murder! And I think you birds know more than you're telling."

Doc Savage said half a dozen words in the guttural Mayan language.

"Here!" ripped Hardboiled. "Speak English!"

Monk and Ham drew air into their lungs, then ceased to

breathe. Doc Savage did likewise. Then the bronze man, without the gesture seeming to mean anything, pressed an elbow tightly to his side.

Hardboiled frowned, his suspicions half aroused, and the frown was still on his leathery forehead, when he drew in a great sobbing breath of air, bent over and peered at the ground as if searching for a suitable resting spot, then laid himself down heavily. He began to snore.

A cop exploded, "Say, what the——" then he, too, dropped. Other policemen around him toppled over. None of them moved after they fell, and all breathed noisily, regularly, in the mysterious stupor which had seized upon them. Only a few snored.

Monk asked, "Any danger of 'em freezing?"

Doc Savage said, "No. They'll wake up in half an hour."

Doc Savage, Monk and Ham departed the spot. Monk and Ham made no comment about what had happened. It was old stuff to them.

Long ago Doc Savage had perfected a gas, odorless and colorless, which produced a quick, temporary unconsciousness and left no harmful aftereffects. The unique thing about this gas was that it became ineffective after somewhat less than a minute. Given a warning, one could evade the gas by holding his breath. The substance, extremely powerful, was carried in small glass bulbs, and the bronze man had broken one of these with elbow pressure.

The three men approached their cars. The pig, Habeas Corpus, had not been close enough to be affected by the anæsthetic, and he now galloped up.

Monk muttered, "I can't stop thinkin' how those men died—with their eyes popping."

Ham, who still clung to his sword cane, said, "What about that Janko Sultman? We know he is mixed up in it. Why don't we get on his neck and make him talk?"

"Pat is working on that," Doc told him. "Something may turn up at the Association of Physical Health."

Chapter VI

PAT HITS A SNAG

Something had turned up at the Association of Physical Health. At least the elevator boy, after his passenger had alighted, twisted his lip distastefully and said over his shoulder, "Now ain't *that* something!"

The "something" was a lissome young man in evening clothes. He had remarkably fragile features and a rose petal skin. There was a gardenia in his lapel, the aroma of mimosa about him.

The newcomer went directly to the receptionist-telephone girl's desk. The blonde was no longer there. A rather dowdy-looking girl who wore glasses had taken her place.

"I wish to see Seco Nandez," he advised.

"Who is calling?" asked the standardized receptionist.

"Tell Nandez it is a gentleman sent by J. S.," he directed.

The information was apparently effective, because the young man was directed toward a door which bore the legend:

SENOR SECO NANDEZ, M. D.
Chief Of Medical Staff

Entering, the effeminate young man shut the door carefully at his back, took out a handkerchief and wiped his finger prints off the knob as if it were a habit—he had opened the door by a shove, without touching the knob on the other side.

"Hyah, Nannie," he smiled.

Seco Nandez scowled at the flippancy. He was a tall, reedy dark man who wore a rather light suit for so late in the Fall. The pallor of the suit emphasized the darkness of Seco Nandez, and his large eyes and thick lips lent a suspicion that some of his ancestors had come from Africa.

"Why do you come here, Lizzie?" he demanded. *"Eso es muy mal!"*

"What's that last?" demanded the young man addressed as "Lizzie."

"It is dangerous," snapped Seco Nandez, putting his Spanish into English.

"Sultman sent me," said Lizzie.

Nandez spread his hands. "But why he not come himself, señor?"

"Trouble with his feet," said Lizzie.

Nandez scowled his puzzlement. "You mean the fallen arches like that so very tough cop, Hardboiled Humbolt? I did not know Sultman had such trouble."

"It's the cold," grinned Lizzie. "Not his arches."

"A hot bath is good for that," Nandez said seriously.

Lizzie laughed sarcastically. "It's right over your head, isn't it, Nannie? You no savvy. Well, a hot bath won't help this kind of cold feet."

"What do you mean, señor?" Nandez questioned sharply.

"Sultman's feet began to cool off when Doc Savage barged in here this afternoon," Lizzie explained. "The temperature took another big drop when that bullet bounced off Sultman's fuzzy head. Boke was responsible for that shooting and Sultman knows it."

Nandez nodded slowly. "*Si, si,* this thing, she is getting very dangerous."

"You knew it would get dangerous when you started it," Lizzie snorted.

Nandez groaned, "It would not, had we but done what Boke hired us to do, and let it go at that. But no, when Sultman learned what Boke planned, he decided to get in ahead of Boke and put the plan through himself."

Lizzie laughed again. His face, his body, were both fragile looking, but there was a hard recklessness in his manner.

"Don't let it get to your feet," he advised. "Hell! There's more money than any of us ever saw in this thing. Boke expected to clean up a billion. I think he was a piker."

Nandez frowned at his manicured, dark fingers. "Do not worry about what you call—my feet."

"Swell!" said Lizzie. "Now, I came to tell you to meet Sultman. We're taking cover from now on, see."

Nandez waved an arm. "But what about the Association of Physical Health?"

"Sultman is just walking off and leaving it," Lizzie grinned. "The damned place ain't making money, anyhow."

"Where is Sultman?" asked Nandez.

"The usual place," advised the other.

Lizzie went to the door, took out his handkerchief and dropped it over the doorknob before he turned it. He waved his free hand airily. "Keep your chin up, Nannie."

Nandez snapped, "Stop calling me that name! I do not like it!"

"There's a lot of things you'd like less," Lizzie grinned, and went out.

Lizzie smiled widely and winked at the little receptionist as he went out. He swung girlishly into the elevator and the cage sank.

The receptionist at the telephone switchboard came to life. Open before her lay a stenographic notebook, its pages covered with expert shorthand pen strokes.

Translated, these shorthand notes would give an exact record of what had been said between Lizzie and Nandez.

The unimpressive young woman removed the telephone headset. Instead of having a single receiver, as was customary, this headset was double and the extra receiver was connected to a circuit of concealed microphones which had been planted in the offices early in the evening during the time the others were dining.

The Association of Physical Health, which gained its revenue from the mere giving of physical examinations, remained open regularly in the evenings to accommodate office workers and those who could not come during daylight hours.

The plain-looking receptionist smiled widely and put the notebook in a hand bag which also held a weapon which resembled an oversized automatic, two extra curled magazines for the gun, a fountain pen tear-gas gun, and a compact. Then the young woman busied herself at the switchboard.

At that point, Seco Nandez came out of his office. He had donned his hat and overcoat and seemed bound on a definite errand as he took the elevator.

The receptionist motioned to a nurse, said, "Take my place, please," and hurried away before the nurse could open her mouth. The young woman ran down the stairs, past where the gunman had been seized with the weird pop-eyed death earlier in the day, and into the lobby.

She ran behind the cigar counter and exchanged her colorless and rather threadbare coat for an exquisite affair of fur. She kicked off her flat-heeled, conservative shoes and donned a pair with high heels, then added a small metallic hat to the outfit.

She used lipstick and rouge expertly. She peeled off a wig of dun-colored hair which she was wearing and replaced it with one of metallic blondness.

The young woman's own hair, it could be observed, was a remarkable bronze hue.

The result of her changes was something of a miracle. The young woman who walked out of the building on the trail of Seco Nandez was a ravishing beauty. Even her carriage was different, the high heels making her look inches taller. If Seco Nandez or Lizzie had met her face to face, it was doubtful if they would have recognized her.

A close acquaintance, however, might have recognized the young woman as Patricia Savage.

Seco Nandez, moving along the gloomy streets, bending over against the pluck of the cold Fall wind, looked back numerous times, but thanks to Pat's skill, noticed nothing unusual, or if he did observe anything, he gave no sign.

His route took him to the east, where the streets became narrow and dark and full of smells and the small drifts of hard white snow, snuggled in bunches behind obstructions, seemed strangely out of place amid the grime and squalor.

There were few persons abroad, which made Pat's job of trailing much simpler; she did not follow abreast of Nandez, but paralleled his course on the next street, watching for him at intersections. There finally came a time when he did not appear at a corner.

Pat hurried down the side street. Her coat collar was upturned, her head down, apparently in defense against the chill wind, but actually to watch the sidewalk. The hard snow, almost like ice pellets, had not covered the walk, but it had eddied into doorways and stoops.

Seco Nandez had turned into a shabby building which was reached by half a dozen stone steps, deeply pitted.

Pat went up the steps boldly, found the door unlocked, and eased inside. Listening, she detected voices muttering from above. One of the speakers was Seco Nandez.

"Listen, chief," Nandez was saying, "you've got to give me time. This fellow Sultman is too slick. We can't hang the goods on him all at once."

Pat heard the words distinctly, but the reply was a monotonous mutter which she could neither understand nor identify.

"The first thing we've got to do," Seco Nandez continued, "is to find where Sultman is hiding. I think I know. I'll go there, then make a report."

This information gave Pat Savage a surprise. Was it possible that she had uncovered a minor double-cross among the ranks of the schemers? Was Nandez on the side of Sultman, or aiding the mysterious Boke?

The unintelligible mutter was replying to Nandez.

"Let's not talk so loud, señor," said Nandez.

After that the voice dropped to complete inaudibility, and Pat, disgusted, mounted the stairs cautiously in order to get nearer and hear better. At the top she found a long corridor which ended, it seemed, in another stairway leading downward to a back door. It was very dark, the passage being unlighted, and Pat felt along with her hands. She located a door.

She could hear no speaking beyond the door. She leaned an ear against the ancient planks. As if that were a signal, motion exploded in the darkness beside her.

Hands seized her throat and her hair, yanked forcibly and unbalanced her. Before she could do a thing about it, she was slammed heavily on the floor.

Seco Nandez, gripping her fiercely, said, "You fall for the trick like the ton of bricks, señorita."

Pat knew the man with whom she fought was her master in physical strength, so instead of wrestling with him, she kicked his shins with the sharp toes of her slippers, hit him on the windpipe, which happens to be a particularly vulnerable part of the human anatomy, and gave one of his ears a terrific twist.

Finally, she managed to execute an ancient and effective bit of rough-and-tumble strategy—she inserted her little finger in Seco Nandez's left nostril and lifted.

Nandez moaned, his moan became a howl, and he floundered in his haste to get erect and away from the torturing finger. He jumped back, slapping his aching proboscis, hissing expletives in Spanish.

Pat did not try to get erect, but rolled over, grabbed her purse and tore it open. The supermachine pistol fell out.

Nandez leaped forward and kicked at the gun. He missed. Pat tried to thumb the safety off. Nandez kicked again, and missed a second time. Then Pat did get the safety off and the gun began to moan like a big bullfiddle and spew empties, but the slugs, going past Nandez, tore plaster off the walls.

Pat corrected her aim; once more Nandez kicked. He was in time. The heavy weapon caromed from wall to floor and Pat groaned and snapped her bruised fingers.

As Nandez fell upon her, she dived her left hand into the purse and got the tear-gas gun. Nandez must have made the mistake of thinking there would be no other weapon in the bag.

Pat jammed the gun into his face, shut her eyes, held her breath and pulled the trigger. The fountain-pen-like barrel made considerable noise and kicked heavily, for the muzzle was against Nandez's skin.

Nandez began to cry out and roll on the floor, and Pat gaining her feet with her eyes still closed, ran for the door. She missed the aperture, smacked a wall, fell over a chair, keeping her eyes shut all of the time, and not breathing, then found the door and went through.

She narrowly missed falling head over heels down the

stairs, and not until she was near the bottom did she open her eyes. She popped outside, only to have a hand clamp her arm.

"Not so fast, sister," said the voice of the feminine-mannered Lizzie.

Pat stood perfectly still, for there was a flat automatic in Lizzie's other hand and the hard bravado of a killer in his strange, limpid eyes.

"Good thing I shagged along behind Nannie," Lizzie said dryly. "What'd you do to him?"

"Let me go!" Pat snapped.

"Sure," said Lizzie, and released her arm.

Then, so suddenly that Pat had no time to dodge, Lizzie struck her with the automatic. He hit with blinding speed, and accurately, with the manner of a man who had done the thing before.

Pat's head filled with a roaring; scarlet curtains fell and rolled before her eyes and black masses came up and danced on the curtains. After that there was a singing sound as of millions of grasshoppers traveling, which resolved into pulsations that in turn became the banging of her pulse.

All the time she was conscious of being handled, and when she opened her eyes, she was upstairs and on the floor, bound and gagged.

Seco Nandez was erect before her, speaking his feelings slowly and painfully, not using particularly vile Spanish words, but putting a great deal of emphasis upon them. The left side of his face was not pleasant to look at, for the tear-gas gun had blown a rather nasty pit. It was still running a little red, and his eyes were streaming tears that mixed and thinned the scarlet fluid.

It was obvious that Nandez could not yet see.

Perhaps ten minutes passed, Lizzie spending the interim in going over the contents of Pat's hand bag and in inspecting the supermachine pistol. Nandez mopped at his face and finally began to see a little.

He snarled when he saw Pat, and grabbed the supermachine pistol from Lizzie.

"Here! Hell!" Lizzie barked; and they struggled over the gun, Nandez grating, "I shall kill her for what she do to me, señor!"

"Use your head," Lizzie snapped.

Nandez continued struggling, managed to get the gun, tried to shoot Pat, and the safety baffled him. He cursed and hurled the weapon with great violence at her head. His aim was very bad; the gun hit the wall, bounced and came to rest so close that Pat instantly rolled in a furious effort to reach it.

Lizzie ran over, put his foot on her and held her stationary.

"What a doll!" he grinned at Pat. "Where do *you* hook into this?" So that she could answer, he removed the gag.

Pat said, "I don't know what this is all about. I came into this building to see a friend, and as I was walking down the corridor that man"—she jerked her head at Nandez—"that man seized me."

"Beautiful!" said Lizzie. "An excellent lie! A gorgeous lie! You're Doc Savage's cousin and you bribed that dizzy blonde at the Association of Physical Health to let you take her place. I've read of you, sister. You're supposed to be good and I guess you really are."

Nandez had sobered. "This señorita, she is connected with Doc Savage?" he demanded.

"She is," said Lizzie. "And that makes it bad. How'd you come to pull in here? This isn't Sultman's hangout."

"I saw her trailing me," said Nandez.

Lizzie put weight on the foot which bore on Pat's back. "How much have you learned, good-looking?"

"Nothing," said Pat.

"That's probably a lie, but it's swell," Lizzie grinned. He looked at Nandez. "You want the job, Nannie?"

"Yes," said Nandez. "And I do not like that nickname, señor."

Lizzie laughed and went out.

Pat knew they must have agreed on her fate during the black period when she had been stunned from the blow on the head.

Nandez drew out a pocketknife, not a large knife, but one with a blade which looked razor sharp.

Lizzie, appearing in the door suddenly, said, "Better wait until that face stops bleeding. You'd make a hell of a spectacle on the street now."

"*Si,*" growled Nandez.

Lizzie, turning, said, "Watch the finger prints, Nannie," and departed once more.

Nandez scowled at the door for a time; then noting that his features no longer oozed scarlet, got to his feet, holding the knife lightly between his fingers.

He advanced with the quick purpose of a man who intended to get it over with.

Pat, suddenly frozen with horror, tried to scream, but the effort was pitifully inadequate—a small whining.

"No one can hear that," said Nandez, and bent down.

Chapter VII

SURPRISE SHADOW

Nandez was wrong in surmising no one would hear the screams. Lizzie heard them. But Lizzie was across the street, and he was listening for them.

The shrill, piping cries that came from the old building might have been the product of the icy Fall wind. But not so the cries which suddenly followed.

Screams broke out, awful, penetrating bleats, full of the grisly quality of death.

"The damned girl should have been gagged!" Lizzie gritted. He started to cross the street. Then he shrank back.

A policeman had appeared, a big, burly cop, bundled to his red ears in his Winter overcoat. He had heard the shrieks and was running. He popped into the building. The shrieks had ceased.

Lizzie swore savagely and dragged out his gun.

"Damn all cops!" he snarled, and whipped across the street. He did not enter, but paused outside, listening. There was a chance that Nandez had fled by the back route.

Lizzie heard the policeman swear in a loud, startled voice. Then feet banged on the stairs. Lizzie retreated hurriedly and was concealed in a near-by doorway before the officer appeared.

The cop did not look around, which surprised Lizzie as well as relieved him no little. The officer ran for a corner, and Lizzie, craning his neck, saw the man using a call box frantically.

"Nandez got away," Lizzie grinned, and used his ears again.

Once he thought he heard movement from the rear of the building, a squeaking sound as of rubber pressing hard against iron or concrete; or it might have been a foot on a board.

"Nandez," Lizzie breathed, and himself eased away from the vicinity.

Lizzie walked hurriedly eastward until he came to a street where, despite the cold of the Fall night, a few persons were abroad, and an occasional taxi prowled. Even then, he did not take a cab, because drivers have memories. He mingled with the crowd and drifted to the nearest subway.

As far as he could tell, he was not followed.

Back in the street, the policeman had deserted his call box. He strode to the building and went inside, only to reappear shortly, mopping his forehead, a strange expression on his features. He waited, consulting his watch.

A faint squealing noise arose in the distance, loudened and became the wail of a siren. The car, a big phaeton, careened into the street and screamed its tires on the pavement as it came to a stop.

In the rear of the phaeton, Hardboiled Humbolt kicked a robe from around his big stockinged feet, grimaced as he drew on his canvas sneakers, and got out, muttering, "It's gettin' damned cold for these canvas shoes."

The patrolman ran up. He jerked a thumb over his shoulder, shouted, "It's in there!"

Hardboiled put a jaw out against the cold gale. "Dead?"

"Dead as can be," said the patrolman. "It's awful!"

"So is about half of this police business," Hardboiled growled, and went inside and up the creaking stairs. He said nothing more, but took a flashlight from his pocket and went into the room. He ranged the flash beam for some seconds over the chamber, but giving most of the time to the corpse on the floor.

The cadaver was a gruesome sight.

Stepping back, Hardboiled picked up a hand bag. He looked inside. There were cards in a pocket; they bore the name of Patricia Savage, the name of her beauty parlor and gymnasium on Park Avenue, and the address.

"Pat Savage," Hardboiled muttered. "She's Doc Savage's cousin."

"Helps him out sometimes on his jobs," said the patrolman. "Or so I've heard."

"She was a lot of help here," Hardboiled said grimly.

The burly police inspector took another turn of the room, using his flashlight, then shook his head and walked out and down the stairs.

"It gets me," he said slowly. "I can't make heads or tails of this whole mess. Send for the medical examiner."

He walked to the phaeton, paused and added, "And spread the net for Doc Savage. Put every radio car in the city to looking for him. That bronze guy knows something he's not telling."

The patrolman took up a position in the corridor. He had found the lights, and he turned them on now; the light seemed to relieve his mind.

Once he thought he heard a sound from within the room where the body lay and he opened the door; but saw no one. After that, he closed the door, as if to keep the grisly presence from within out of his thoughts.

The door had not been closed for long when the window lifted slightly. It was the first rise of the window which had attracted the officer's attention.

A great, shadowy figure eased into the room. A flashlight beam no larger than a pencil came into being and raced about, resting finally on the body and roaming over it slowly.

The body was twisted, as if it had fallen in the throes of awful agony. The face was pocked deeply on one side by a burn, and the lips were bitten and redstained.

The eyes were barely in their sockets, having squeezed out as if propelled by some inner force. The muscles attached to them were gray and horrible.

The giant prowler bent over the form and a hand roved, exploring pockets. Once the hand got in the way of the thin light beam, and it could be seen that the skin was an unusual bronze color, and the hands had tremendous tendons. Letters yielded Seco Nandez's name.

Next, the bronze man examined the purse of Patricia Savage, where it had been replaced on the floor.

There was no sound audible as the metallic giant went to the window, eased through and put his weight on the fire escape outside. He went down to the landing, grasped a silken cord which was attached to a collapsible grappling hook and slid down into the alley below. A flip of the cord brought the grapple down, and the bronze man stowed it within his clothing.

He joined two figures waiting silently in the darkness.

Monk, with the pig, Habeas Corpus, silent under an arm, asked, "What did you find, Doc?"

"A pop-eyed dead man named Seco Nandez," Doc Savage said. "And Pat's purse was near by."

"Strange," murmured the dapper Ham. "Something has happened here."

From the near-by darkness, Pat's voice stated, "You said it!"

Monk started, all but dropping Habeas, and Ham instinctively whipped up his sword cane. Doc Savage showed no perceptible surprise.

Patricia Savage came from the gloom.

"I have been hanging around," she said. "I had an idea you would show up here."

"We're in bad with the police," Monk told her. "But we had our radio tuned on the police radio station and heard the call which brought Hardboiled Humbolt here. We dropped in to see what it was all about."

Doc Savage asked, "What happened, Pat?"

Pat was a young woman of crisp explanations. There was no tremble, no excitement in her voice as she summarized what had happened from the time she had overheard the conversation of Seco Nandez and Lizzie at the Association of Physical Health. She brought the narrative down to its gory climax.

"This Nandez was just leaning over to use his knife," she said. "He was a killer who enjoyed it. I could see that in his eyes. He held my nose to stop what little noise I was able to make, and bent my head back. Then—something happened."

"The pop-eyed death?" Doc asked.

"He began to scream," Pat said, her voice suddenly thin. "And his eyes—they—it was awful!"

"We seen it happen to a whole roomful of men at once," Monk muttered.

Ham clicked his sword cane nervously.

"Doc, this thing is incredible!" he snapped. "It is as if some supernatural power were striking down these men in the act of doing murder. What do you think the pop-eyed death is?"

Monk added, "And what makes it get 'em only when they're about to kill somebody? Or right after they've killed?"

There was a long pause while they waited for Doc Savage to make an answer, and when he did not, and gave no sign of intending to do so, Pat broke the tension.

"I used Nandez's knife and cut myself loose after he—died," she said. "I got to the rear stairway and ran down it, not knowing but that Nandez's partner, Lizzie, might come back."

"And you waited here," Ham finished.

"Hold on," said Pat. "I want to tell you about something queer that happened down here in the alley."

"What?" Doc questioned.

"Some one came out."

"Maybe it was the policeman looking around?" Doc offered.

Pat shook a vehement negative. "No. It was a giant figure of a man—a fellow I will swear was almost as large as you, Doc. And he moved like a ghost. He came down the fire escape."

"Down the fire escape?" Monk grunted.

"Exactly," said Pat. "It looked as if he had been outside of the window all of the time."

"You did not see him clearly?" Doc questioned.

"Too dark," said Pat. "And he traveled like a black ghost."

Monk snorted suddenly. "Did you hear his feet on the fire escape? I mean—did they make squeaking sounds?"

"Why, now that you mention it, I think they did," Pat murmured.

Ham growled, "What are you getting at, you homely monkey?"

Doc Savage answered that.

"Monk was thinking of canvas-soled rubber shoes," the bronze man said. "Rubber squeaks sometimes when it is rubbed over iron."

Ham began, "But what——" then fell silent. He had thought of Hardboiled Humbolt and his rubber-soled canvas shoes.

Some moments later Doc Savage, Monk, Ham and Pat were in a sedan traveling a near-by street.

"We dropped in at headquarters and exchanged the roadster and the coupé for this bus," Monk explained. "The cops were looking for the other two cars."

"And saw a flock of policemen watching the place for us," Ham added.

Pat watched the darkened houses slip by and shivered.

"The police are against us," she said softly. "One of our men has been murdered, and we can't find Robert Lorrey. And some infernal death is striking. This is more than I bargained for."

"Want to lay off?" Doc asked. "You'd better."

"Don't be silly," said Pat. "What do we do next?"

"Since our headquarters are watched, we will make use of Renny's apartment," Doc said.

Colonel John Renwick, the engineer of Doc's group, was a gentleman who had made some millions in his profession, prior to his affiliation with high adventure in the person of the bronze man. He still commanded staggering fees when he worked.

Renny occupied a penthouse overlooking Central Park. The building, one of the most flamboyant in the city, was one

Renny had designed and the erection of which he had supervised, and his apartment was an incredible array of modernistic metals and glass. Mechanical gadgets were everywhere, and the wide, glass-covered terrace was a greenhouse of tropical shrubs.

Renny, they found on arrival, was not present. Doc had a key and they entered.

"Wonder what's become of Renny?" Monk pondered. "Reckon the bigfisted lummox got that message you left on the office window?"

Doc Savage neglected to answer, for he was picking up a telephone. He got in communication with each of the city's large broadcasting stations in succession and spoke rapidly. Hanging up after communicating with the first one, he went over and switched on a large modernistic radio.

A dance orchestra was playing, and the tone of Renny's radio speaker was an acoustic engineer's dream come to life. But almost at once, the strains were interrupted.

"An announcement of importance," said the announcer. "Will No. 17 get in touch with his chief. And will No. 17 guard his own life carefully and communicate with no one but his chief. For No. 17's benefit, Leander Court was murdered to-day."

The orchestra strains resumed, and Doc Savage tuned in on another station and shortly got almost the identical announcement.

No. 17 was Robert Lorrey—the number he bore on Doc Savage's pay roll.

The fact that the bronze man had been able to prevail upon every broadcasting station to insert such an unusual announcement in the regular evening routine was an indication of his influence.

"I hope," Monk said, "that Robert Lorrey turns up before long."

Chapter VIII

THE CRIME GLAND

At that precise instant, but quite a few blocks distant from Renny's sumptuous penthouse, the lissome and feminine-mannered Lizzie was listening to a worried voice come from an adjacent room.

"I hope Robert Lorrey shows up soon," it said.

Lizzie shrugged. He had changed his evening garb for full dress, perfect in its every detail, and he had even less the appearance of a cold-blooded criminal who not long before had left a companion to cut the throat of a young woman.

Janko Sultman was walking circles in the next room. He still wore his loud-checked suit, and there was a bandage stuck in the midst of his upstanding, frizzled hair with adhesive tape. From time to time he fingered this bandage.

"Dot Boke!" he growled. "If der bullet had come another inch lower, it would have meant finish for me."

Lizzie carefully adjusted the hang of the bright chain which spanned the front of his waistcoat.

"Give me a line on this Boke, and I'll soon stop him," he said lazily.

Janko Sultman waved plump hands. "It's a swell idea, only it's no good."

"Why not?"

"I do not know dot Boke by sight, or where to find him."

"The hell you don't!" Lizzie snorted. "Then how did you contact him in the first place?"

"Through a witch-faced feller dot was called Frightful," explained Sultman. "They had figured dot because I was a doctor, I should be able to get a line on Doc Savage's place where he fixed up der crooks. But this Frightful did all der talking. Not once did I see Boke. I hear him over der telephone, though, and he have the sweetest voice you ever listen to."

"He's got sweet ways, too," grinned Lizzie, casting a glance at Sultman's bandaged head. "And the guy Frightful was found dead in that roomful of men who had their eyes popping. The newspapers are full of it."

"Dot's another thing!" Sultman wailed. "The eye-popping business! What is it? She gets my goat!"

A man appeared at the door and said, "Robert and Sidney Lorrey calling."

Janko Sultman looked very pained and swore. "Dot fool brought his brother!"

Lizzie asked, "Well, they've been going around together since you kindly gave Robert his vacation." Then Lizzie laughed. "I waonder if Doc Savage has found out about those faked telegrams yet?"

Sultman waved his arms. "Damn it, we've got to get rid of Sidney. I cannot buy them both."

Lizzie grinned, "Leave it to me," and started for the door.

Sultman gulped, "Listen, what——"

"Give me five minutes," Lizzie requested. "I'll fix it."

Then he went out.

Janko Sultman hastily summoned three men into the room. They were smooth-looking gentlemen who might have been bank clerks reporting for a day's work, except that each had a submachine gun tucked under an arm.

"Robert Lorrey will be here soon," Janko Sultman said. "I cannot afford to take any chances."

One of the smooth-looking men nodded. "You think he may jump you?" he asked.

"Not so much dot," said Sultman. "But when he learns why he has been summoned here, he may fly off der handle, as did Leander Court, and threaten to go to Doc Savage. He must be prevented from doing dot."

"Sure," said one of the men. "Only I hope we don't get the same dose as the guy you posted to get Leander Court if he went up in the air. That bird died with his eyes sticking out."

"Don't be silly!" Sultman snapped. "There is no one around here who can touch you. The gunman dot shot Court merely had some kind of a spasm."

"How about the whole roomful of pop-eyed dead the papers are playing up, then?" countered the other.

"Let it go!" Sultman groaned. "Hurry. I will hide you."

The room was paneled with wood; there were many pictures, all of excellent taste. Sultman crossed the deep carpet, a grotesque figure with his frizzled hair, and opened a wall panel. There was a recess behind large enough to hold a man, and a lookout standing within could peer into the room through an ingenious colored screen which was a part of a picture fastened on the outside. One of the men with machine guns was posted inside.

There proved to be two more niches, and additional guards were posted in these.

"Dot is good," Sultman decided.

The three gunmen, looking through loopholes, had only to move their heads to get a full view of the room. The picture was fairly distinct, although colors were distorted by the pigment of the screen through which they had to peer.

A few seconds later, Janko Sultman was shaking hands with a lean, stoopshouldered man, and the latter was admitting, "Yes. I am Robert Lorrey."

Robert Lorrey was an extremely plain man as far as outward appearances went. He had mouse-colored hair and eyes which were pale, but which were also made slightly grotesque by the powerful lenses of the spectacles which he wore. Pressing would have helped his gray suit, and he was bundled to the ears in a fuzzy woolen muffler.

"This is my brother Sidney," said Robert Lorrey.

"Ah, yes," said Sultman, lying smoothly. "Some one told me you had a brother. Twins, aren't you?"

This last was a rank guess on the frizzled-haired man's part, for Sidney was a smaller carbon copy of his brother, although he did have an unnaturally high forehead in addition. It was possible that Sidney looked a bit more the idealist, the dreamer.

"We are twins," Robert agreed. "I hope you do not mind my bringing Sidney along. We are very fond of each other, and we frequently coöperate in conducting experiments."

"As a matter of fact, my brother has financed most of my experiments," said Sidney.

"You are welcome, of course," Janko Sultman lied.

The telephone rang.

Sultman looked surprised, went over to the instrument and answered. He was not a very good actor, for he failed to keep pleasure off his features.

"For Sidney Lorrey," he said.

Sidney Lorrey spoke for a few minutes over the line, and there was a puzzled expression on his features as he put the instrument down.

"I shall have to go," he said. "Some one wants to speak to me. He says it is very important."

Sidney Lorrey took his departure.

Janko Sultman now became the perfect host, offering Robert Lorrey fine cigars and excellent liquor, both of which the stoop-shouldered, mouse-like man turned down, explaining that he did not imbibe.

"The result of Doc Savage's training, eh?" murmured Sultman dryly. "The bronze man is quite a puritan, I've heard."

Robert Lorrey became very quiet in his chair. He plucked at the ends of his burry muffler.

"You have evidently made a mistake," he said shortly. "I scarcely know this Doc Savage—if I am to presume that when you say Doc Savage, you mean the remarkable bronze man who has become noted as a man who gets others out of trouble."

Janko Sultman laughed. "Dere is no use of pretending between friends."

"I scarcely know you," Robert Lorrey pointed out.

Sultman pretended not to hear the last reminder.

"I know many things," he smiled. "I know, for instance, dot Doc Savage is a man who does peculiar things. One of the most peculiar of these things, perhaps, is his habit of sending criminals whom he catches to a weird institution which he maintains in upstate New York."

Robert Lorrey said sharply, "If you assume I know all of this, you are wrong."

"The criminals undergo a treatment which causes them to lose their memories, and to become honest men," continued Sultman. "Strange as it sounds, dot is what happens."

"I do not care to hear more about this!" snapped Robert Lorrey. "The whole thing sounds ridiculous!"

Janko Sultman carefully adjusted the bandage on top of his head then lighted himself a cigar, at the same time never taking his eyes from his visitor.

"Doc Savage has seized many criminals during his career," Sultman went on. "This Savage is a remarkable individual, more remarkable than most persons can realize. He is almost a mental freak. His knowledge in der fields of electricity, chemistry and engineering and so on is profound. But greatest of all is his skill as a surgeon."

Lorrey moistened his lips. "Why are you telling me this?"

Janko Sultman seemed not to hear. "Doc Savage has discovered dot crime is, in a sense, a disease," he went on. "In other words, we will take for der purpose of illustration, de effect of ordinary inflammation on tonsils. If a man has infected tonsils, a toxic poison gradually filters from them through his system, and his nerves are affected, so dot he becomes irritable. He gets der jitters. He is hard to get along with."

"You do not need to be so elementary," snapped Robert Lorrey.

"Sure," Sultman smiled. "There are many glands in the human body. They secrete everything from perspiration to digestive juices. Many of them are in the human brain, and it is these last that are the least known."

"What has this to do with crime as a disease?" Lorrey interrupted.

"There is a small gland which governs operation of a certain section of der brain which controls a human being's behavior," said Sultman. "If dot gland is out of order, der patient loses his sense of right and wrong. In other words, he gets so he does not give a damn what happens or what he does. Doc Savage has discovered this."

"I would not call that one of Doc Savage's discoveries," Robert Lorrey put in. "Many criminologists have arrived at that conclusion."

Sultman shrugged. "Anyway, Doc Savage straightens up dot gland at his place in upstate New York, and dot is what makes honest men of the crooks. Of course, he severs certain nerves in their brains, too, which makes them forget their past."

"This is quite amazing," said Robert Lorrey.

"No it isn't," grinned Sultman. "You know all about it, because you are one of der men who do der operating on crooks."

The three gunmen, watching from their concealed niches, saw from Robert Lorrey's sudden tensing that he was shocked by the disclosure that another man knew of his profession.

They heard Lorrey bark, "How did you learn this? No one is supposed to know."

They saw Janko Sultman puff at his cigar, then draw his chair closer to that of Robert Lorrey, ignoring Lorrey's tendency to shrink away from him. There was a smug look on Sultman's face, and one gunman reflected that he looked like a fuzzy-haired cannibal about to indulge in a meal.

Janko Sultman now began speaking rapidly, but his words did not reach the guards, for they were pitched low. The watchers could only observe the play of emotions on the features of Robert Lorrey.

Lorrey at first registered surprise, then that became a shocked, blank look, and as Sultman went on speaking, amazement, wonder and horror followed each other successively. Then rage blazed in the meek-looking scientist's eyes.

"You go to hell!" he yelled, and sprang to his feet.

Sultman dropped his cigar and scrambled erect, yelling, "Don't be a fool! I'll raise the ante! I'll make it a hundred thousand dollars!"

"No!" snapped Lorrey.

"A quarter of a million!" Sultman offered desperately.

"No!"

"Fifty per cent of all we can take in!"

"I told you to go to hell!" Robert Lorrey shouted. Then he backed toward the door.

Sultman stepped hastily aside and snapped, "Don't let him out, men!"

"He won't leave," Lizzie said unexpectedly from the door.

Lizzie had come back silently, and it was evident that he did not know Janko Sultman had posted gunmen behind the wall panels.

Robert Lorrey turned around and saw the flat automatic which Lizzie was holding in one girlishly small hand. He put his own hands up.

Sultman asked Lizzie, "You got rid of Sidney Lorrey?"

Lizzie laughed. "I didn't have to. I just told him over the telephone when I called here that I had some important information for him. I made an appointment in a drug store far enough away so that he won't get back in time to bother us."

Robert Lorrey swallowed rapidly. "What are you going to do with me?"

"I was forced to have your superior, Leander Court, killed," Sultman smiled. "I will not make that mistake again. We will use other means on you."

"What do you mean?" Lorrey snapped.

"You are going to be persuaded to do as I wish," advised Sultman. "I have thought it all out very carefully."

"Including what Doc Savage will do to you if you harm me?" asked Lorrey.

Janko Sultman looked as if some one had jabbed him unexpectedly with a pin. But the expression was fleeting.

"I am not afraid of Doc Savage," he growled. "You might as well make up your mind that you are going to do the thing I wish."

Robert Lorrey's answer was to dive suddenly at Lizzie's gun. The wielder of the weapon was taken by surprise and permitted the stoop-shouldered man to get a grip on it. Lorrey kicked Lizzie's shins from under him. The man, falling, released his weapon.

Janko Sultman, forgetting he had the gunmen posted back of the wall panels, ran and leaped upon Robert Lorrey. Stunned, Lorrey lost his weapon.

Lizzie got up snarling and snatched a long stiletto from inside his immaculate full dress garb. He started for Robert Lorrey—and stopped.

Lizzie put a hand up to his eyes. They were protruding a little. He dropped his knife.

"My head!" he wailed horribly. "My eyes! Something is wrong——"

Lizzie had shut the door when he came inside, but now there was a loud crash and an explosion of splinters. A second crash followed. A fist—an incredible fist that looked

like the business end of a circus stake-driver's maul—was
smashing through the panel. The door collapsed.

The man who came through was a tower of bone and
gristle.

Robert Lorrey looked at the newcomer, wide-eyed and
startled.

"Renny!" he shouted delightedly.

Chapter IX

BOKE'S TOUCH

Renny looked over the room and the expression on his long,
puritanical face was one of absolute gloom—an indication
that he was enjoying himself, for, adversely, the sadder Renny looked, the more interest he was taking in proceedings.

He was a giant, this Renny, weighing near two hundred
and sixty pounds, most of it bone, a little gristle, and not
much else. Yet, huge as he was, the proportions of his fists
were such as to make the rest of him seem inadequately
small. Each was composed of near a half gallon of bone and
tendon.

Lizzie was still swaying, pawing at his face, his eyes. He
had not fallen, and he seemed to be recovering a little from
the effects of the strange spell which had seized upon him.

"The pop-eyed death," Sultman choked, eying his aide.

Robert Lorrey also fell to studying Lizzie. There was a
professional curiosity in his scrutiny.

"Where did you first feel pain?" he asked. "And was there
any sensation prior to the pain?"

Lizzie was too occupied with his own difficulties to answer.

Renny, moving across the floor with an ease unusual for so
big a man, scooped up all of the weapons in sight. This
caused Sultman to retreat and furtively eye the panels behind
which his machine gunners were concealed.

Catching a moment when Renny and Lorrey were not
looking. Sultman shook his head violently, admonishing the
gunners not to fire.

Robert Lorrey asked Renny, "How on earth did you get
here?"

The big-fisted engineer looked very gloomy.

"There was a message at Doc's office," he offered in a

whooping, roaring voice. "It outlined what had happened. I couldn't locate Doc, so I thought I'd keep an eye on Pat. The message told where she was."

Lizzie stopped feeling of his eyes, which were almost normal again, and glared at Renny.

The big-fisted engineer jingled the weapons in his enormous digits.

"Pat didn't know I was looking out for her," he went on. "I kept in the background, and when she followed Seco Nandez and the sissy here——" he paused to nod at the effeminate Lizzie—"I trailed along. Well, they grabbed Pat, and the pretty boy here left his partner, Nandez, to cut her throat. I was about to interfere when Nandez stuck his eyes out, had a fit and died. I saw Pat was safe, so I left on sissy's trail. I've been hanging around since, trying to get an earful."

Lizzie became slack-jawed. Janko Sultman looked slightly ill. It was the first they had heard of the pop-eyed death of their co-conspirator Seco Nandez, and the news was surprising, not at all pleasant.

Sultman looked at Lizzie and snarled, "You careless drummer! A hell of a mess you have got us into!"

Lizzie said, "Nuts to you!" but he looked worried. He was trying to think how Renny could have followed him so expertly and so unnoticeably, and the upshot of his thinking was that he should have used a great deal more caution.

Renny waved his fistful of weapons and his great voice jumped and thumped in the room.

"Get a move on, boys," he directed. "We're all going to have a talk with Doc Savage."

That made Sultman start and think of his machine gunners behind the wall panels, so he backed slowly to one side until he stood in the clear, then stiffened himself and yelled desperately in command.

"Just the big man!" he howled. "Save Lorrey!"

Renny realized then that there must be some one else concealed around the room. He flopped down to make himself as small a target as possible and bulleted toward the door, his idea being to fight back from the opening. But his precautions were hardly necessary, as it developed.

One of the wall panels snapped open—a necessary move before the men behind could use their guns, for when the panels were closed, there was not room.

The man who came through did not even hold his submachine gun. The weapon lay on the floor of the niche. The man was bent over, and he bent even more, seeming to contort himself in a titanic effort, his face becoming purple with the strain.

As they watched, his eyes came slowly out, like seeds from a purple grape, and it seemed certain they would fall to the floor, but they did not. Then he began to yell in pain.

The other two gunners were crying out too, threshing about, and making awful garglings. One got out of his niche and died on the floor; the other only got the door of his concealment—the wall panel—ajar, and was unable to get out. He convulsed his mortal existence away while curled up in the cramped confines.

Strange things were happening to Lizzie and Janko Sultman, too. Lizzie was having trouble with his eyes again, grasping his head and moaning, and Janko Sultman, for the first time, was standing slightly pop-eyed.

Suddenly Sultman emitted a wail of terror and stampeded for the door, but Renny, who was affected not at all by the pop-eyed spell, mysteriously enough, tripped Sultman and calmly stood on the middle of the man's back.

Renny frowned at the three machine gunners. So amazing was their affliction, so preposterous was the whole thing, that Renny plainly doubted the evidence of his own eyes, or suspected some trick. Finally it dawned on him that this was no trick but death in some grisly, inexplicable form, and the big-fisted engineer voiced a pet exclamation of wonder which he saved for all special occasions.

"Holy cow!" he boomed hoarsely.

Robert Lorrey passed a hand over his forehead and blinked vacantly.

"The most incredible thing I ever saw," he muttered. "What on earth is it?"

Renny did not answer, for there seemed no reply to give. He swallowed several times, then bethought himself of the business at hand and again gathered up guns. He nudged Lizzie and the dazed Sultman, both of whom were still mildly affected by the weird trouble. They stood meekly while he went over their persons, searching for weapons. He even relieved them of their penknives.

"We'll go see Doc Savage now," he advised.

Lizzie and Sultman obeyed like punished children as the big-fisted engineer urged them toward the stairway; they went down slowly, fear making them very silent.

"Their eyes!" Sultman moaned and gave a great shake of a shudder which all but threw him down the steps.

Renny collared the fuzzy-haired man suddenly. "How many more men have you working for you?"

Sultman opened his mouth, and it was plain that he was on the point of giving some number, but he reconsidered, looked sly and said, "No more."

Renny slapped him. The slap was not gentle. It knocked Sultman down the remaining six stairs of the flight.

"I'll knock you out from under that frizzled hair if you start lying to me," the big-fisted engineer promised.

Sultman, lying on the floor, moaned and did not try to get up.

Lizzie snarled, "Keep your hands off Sully!"

Renny turned around and took Lizzie's slim throat in both huge hands, then lifted Lizzie from the floor without apparent difficulty and squeezed a little, tentatively. Lizzie flailed his arms and made froglike noises.

"I haven't forgotten that you walked off callously and left your pal to cut Pat's throat," Renny boomed.

He squeezed again slowly, not relaxing the pressure even when Lizzie squirmed his wildest. Lizzie's face became splotchy, then purple, and his tongue stuck small and pink and straight through his teeth.

Robert Lorrey said nervously, "It is Doc Savage's policy never to take a human life."

"Sure," Renny said. "But mistakes will happen."

Renny looked very sober, with lines about his mouth and a gloomy, almost tearful droop to his eyes.

Janko Sultman got up from the floor, as if he wanted to run, but Renny lashed a foot out and tripped him down again.

Sultman was terrified. He looked at the unlucky Lizzie, and had difficulty getting his breath.

"You were going to take us to Doc Savage," he wailed.

"Sure," Renny said. "But maybe I changed my mind, and decided to make you two talk right here. Who is this Boke, the man with the mysterious voice?"

"I do not know," Sultman moaned. "Dot is the truth."

"What proposition did Boke put up to you through this man, Frightful?" Renny continued.

Sultman looked away and wailed, "You have got me all wrong and dot is a fact."

Robert Lorrey, who had moved toward the door to look out into the darkened street, gave a sudden start and yelled.

Renny, who had been putting on a tough performance merely

in hopes of impressing Sultman and Lizzie to the point where they would break down and unburden their souls of the truth, whirled. He half expected to see Robert Lorrey in the grip of the fantastic pop-eyed death.

What he did see was Robert Lorrey in the grip of a burly, brown-skinned man who had sleek black hair and a remarkably stupid-looking face. This man had succeeded in grabbing a gun which Robert Lorrey chanced to be carrying, and he was endeavoring to drag his captive outside.

Renny emitted a whooping roar and slammed for the door.

Two more men appeared beside the brown-skinned fellow, popping in out of the night. They grabbed Lorrey. Then other men came in behind them, these with guns.

Renny was upon the group now. There was light inside the door, and those who had come in from the night were a little blind, so that the big-fisted engineer's recklessness was justified. He smashed one gunman in the face; the fellow flew back, his features flattened as by the blow of a great maul.

The other man dodged, and Renny's slugging fist only banged the top of his head, which to an ordinary fist would have been more damaging than to the head. But Renny's was no ordinary set of knuckles, and the victim fell as if he had been hit with an iron bar.

The trio seeking to hold Robert Lorrey were brushed aside easily, and before they could help themselves, were hurled out into the street.

In shoving them outside, Renny got a look at the street, distinguishing other shadowy figures there.

"Too many outside!" he rapped. "We'll try the back way."

They ran down the corridor; but long before the rear door was in sight, they heard feet pounding, men grunting, and knew enemies had flanked them, coming in through the rear.

Renny, busy cuffing Sultman and Lizzie along with him, snapped at Robert Lorrey, "Get back!"

"We can get out through a side window," whined Janko Sultman.

Renny scowled darkly at Sultman, then his scowl turned to brisk interest. There was a great fear on the fuzzyhaired man's features.

"Who are these guys jumping us?" Renny demanded.

Sultman wrung his hands.

"Boke's men," he groaned. "They must be!"

Down the passage, coming from the rear door, a single pencil-sized tongue of red flame pumped in the murk. Renny got down fast. The flame spiked again. Gun sound quaked each time.

Renny had turned his shoulder to see if Robert Lorrey, who had retreated a little, was safe. It was a little more luminous where Robert Lorrey stood, and Renny distinctly saw Lorrey's head kick back and a small blue spot appear in the center of his forehead.

Lorrey's knees caved queerly, so that he turned as he fell, and a much larger pit was visible in the back of his cranium where the bullet had come out. His fall was noisy, and only his fingers moved afterward. Their quivering rapidly stilled.

Men with guns now seemed to flow from all sides into the house. They were tall fellows, short men, thin men and broad men. There was some shooting, but that ceased when a low order was passed around.

Renny carried one of the supermachine pistols, and he got a chance to use it, blasting two men down with streams of mercy bullets.

Then some one threw a chair at him, which he ducked, but the chair bounced back from the wall and got in his way as he tried to run across the room. He fell. Men piled on him in a flood. With guns they clubbed his head until it rang. The clubbing made his finger tips tingle and his arms difficult to move.

They tied his ankles and his arms with wire torn from floor lamps, then distended his mouth with the biggest part of a pillow case.

Renny lay there on the floor, looking at his captors, and decided they were a thoroughly hard crew. His inspection made him conscious of the cold which had come in with the opened doors, and he shivered a little.

The men dragged Sultman and Lizzie into the room. Both these two had also been bound and gagged, and they got rough treatment. The bandage had been torn out of Sultman's frizzled hair and the bullet wound was flowing red. A man appropriated Lizzie's watch chain from the front of his dress waistcoat, then calmly tore the pockets out of his garments looking for money. Finding little, he kicked Lizzie in the sides until the pain brought tears to Lizzie's eyes.

Listeners had evidently gone outside, for they now came in to report that the shooting had not attracted attention. Renny, hearing this, was not surprised, for the house was an isolated one and the night itself was noisy.

Robert Lorrey was carried inside, and the men bent over

him anxiously. They cursed when they found the bullet hole through the brain. The violence of their profanity showed they had shot Lorrey by accident.

"A thorough mess!" said a voice. "Yes, a very thorough mess!"

Renny was struck and held by that voice, for it was a tone that was unnaturally pleasant. It had a fascination. One wanted to hear it again. He stared about the room, trying to ascertain who had spoken.

"Things may come out all right after all, however," said the utterly enthralling voice.

Renny shuddered; he could not help it. For that amazing voice seemed to be coming from thin air. It was as if the speaker were invisible.

Chapter X

TORTURE

Sidney Lorrey, twin brother of the unfortunate Robert, had a small habit of tearing matches to pieces with his fingers when he was not mentally at ease. The tiled floor about the chair on which he sat was strewn with flakes of mutilated matchwood.

Sidney Lorrey finished dissecting the last match of the book which had been in the smoking tray on the drug-store table, then stood slowly erect. The store was a small one, with two large telephone booths in the back. Sidney Lorrey went over to the fountain clerk who was pouring steaming water into a coffee percolator.

"A gentleman called me from one of the telephone booths here and asked me to meet him," Lorrey told the clerk. "I don't find any sign of him. Did he leave any message?"

The clerk stopped pouring. "When'd he call you?"

Sidney Lorrey calculated the time since he had left his brother Robert in the company of Janko Sultman.

"Half an hour," he said. "Yes, half an hour ago."

The clerk grinned lopsidedly. "Somebody's been kidding you, brother."

Sidney Lorrey, who did not like to be addressed familiarly, frowned, "What do you mean?"

"Those booths ain't connected," said the clerk. "They're out of order, or something. Go back there and you'll see there's a sign on them that says they won't work. And nobody has called from here to-night."

Sidney Lorrey absently lifted a toothpick off the counter and broke it to pieces. It had just struck him that there was something strange about the call which had come to Janko Sultman's place. He had realized earlier that the voice of the man who had telephoned him had belonged to an entire stranger, and the fact that the fellow had been secretive, saying it was vitally important to see Sidney, but neglecting to convey details, was queer.

But the startling fact, which had just dawned on Sidney Lorrey, was that he had told no one he was going to accompany his brother Robert to Sultman's rendezvous.

Sidney Lorrey and his brother had been eating at a small restaurant which they favored habitually, when Janko Sultman had gotten in touch with Robert and made the appointment.

Sidney Lorrey swung out of the drug store, baffled wrinkles ridging his unnaturally high forehead, popped himself into a taxicab and a few minutes later was alighting in front of Janko Sultman's place. He dismissed the cab, for he presumed his brother was still inside.

He glanced up at the windows of the house. They were curtained, but he thought he saw movement. He drew his coat closer against the chill of this unnatural Fall evening and stepped toward the doorway, being swallowed by the shadows.

In the upstairs room, the man who had looked through the window and seen Sidney Lorrey wheeled on his fellows.

"The brother!" he snapped.

From the adjacent room came the pleasant voice of the mysterious Boke.

"A bit of profound luck, gentlemen," it said.

The other scowled. "Luck! And with his brother lying dead here?"

Boke did not appear, but his voice came plainly.

"Get Sidney," he said. "It may be that he will serve our purpose as well as his brother."

The men in the room moved with swift efficiency. The light was not on in the hallway, nor did they turn any on, but positioned themselves, one on either side of the front door, just inside. They held guns ready in their hands.

A full minute ticked away. The sinister men stirred uneasily, realizing that Sidney Lorrey should have reached the door by now. They allowed more seconds to pass, then pulled the curtain back from the door and peered out into the cold-swept street. After that, they wrenched the door wide and craned their necks up and down the street.

Sidney Lorrey was nowhere in sight.

Upstairs, the strangely attractive voice of Boke was giving quiet orders and men were scampering about making rapid preparations. In the main room, there was still no sign of Boke. His voice came from an adjacent chamber.

One man seemed to be the lieutenant in charge; he came out of the room from which Boke had spoken. His movements were brusque, and an onlooker might have mistaken him for the mysterious Boke—until he spoke. He had a coarse, squeaky voice.

The man's face held satisfaction as they finished their preparations. He backed away, quietly tamping aromatic tobacco into a pipe.

"What do you think of it, Leo?" Boke's voice asked from the adjacent room.

Leo applied tiny flame from a platinum lighter and let the pipe light itself. He did not draw in.

"Swell," he said.

Then Leo's hair all but stood on end. His pipe, lost out of his teeth, hit the floor and showered sparks like a small Vesuvius.

"Do not turn around," advised an utterly cold voice at Leo's back.

The man called Leo did not turn. The others in the room froze and became very careful of what gestures they made with their hands.

Sidney Lorrey had appeared in the door, and he held in one hand a small double-action revolver from which the barrel had been sawed. The calibre of the gun was great—its barrel diameter was such as to almost admit a finger.

"I came in the back way," Sidney Lorrey said dryly. "I do not know who you gentlemen are, or why you were acting so mysteriously. I want my brother."

Leo bowed slightly. He had long black hair and a lock of it fell down over his forehead when he bowed.

"Your brother left here some time ago," he said.

Sidney Lorrey smiled thinly over his revolver.

"There is something very queer going on here," he said. "I can see it in your manner, on your faces."

Leo absently replaced the stray lock of black hair. "When a man walks in on us with a gun, as you have, do you expect us to look blasé about it?"

Sidney Lorrey backed toward the door. These men were dangerous, and there were more of them in the house. He beckoned at Leo with his sawed-off gun.

"I am leaving," he advised. "You will walk downstairs and a short distance from the house with me. If any one menaces me in any way, I shall do my best to blow your spine in two pieces."

Leo's hair seemed to become blacker, his eyes darker, his brows and lashes more smoky, all because his face had turned extremely pale. But he did not resist or say anything, but stepped out into the hallway.

Leo stumbled on the stairs, having difficulty with his feet, and only Sidney Lorrey's hand entangled grimly in the collar of his coat kept him from falling. They passed through the door which gave into an alley full of cold, hard snow particles and darkness.

Some one, leaning from a window directly above the alley door, held a heavy typewriter with both hands. There was enough light that the figures below showed as vague blurs against the snow, and the man let his typewriter drop carefully.

The typewriter carriage slid back with a *ziz-z-z* of a noise as it started to fall, and this caused Sidney Lorrey to look up. He jumped, but not soon enough; the heavy office appliance struck his head. The typewriter bell rang loudly, then rang again as the machine hit the alley pavement. Sidney Lorrey fell atop the typewriter.

Black-haired Leo leaned against the house wall and pounded his chest slowly, as if his heart had almost stopped.

Sidney Lorrey was awakened by the raucous sound of some one telling Leo, "Well, hell, it was all we could do! We figured he wouldn't plug you after the typewriter hit him."

Opening his eyes, Lorrey saw Leo and the other men around him. Leo had recovered his pipe and was puffing it, filling the room with aromatic tobacco fumes. No one seemed to be in a hurry; no one showed particular excitement.

A groan came from a long, boxshaped modernistic divan which stood on the opposite side of the room. Sidney tried to sit up, only to discover he was bound securely, hands and feet held together in one knot of stout cords. He managed to lift his head.

"Bob!" he exploded.

The form of Robert Lorrey reposed on the divan. There

was a bandage over his head, a gag in his mouth. Even as Sidney stared, Robert Lorrey's form stirred slightly to the accompaniment of a second groan.

"Bob!" Sidney gasped. "Are you hurt badly? Are you conscious?"

The head of Robert Lorrey rolled so that Sidney could not see the lips, but he heard a mumble, the words not quite distinguishable.

Then Sidney Lorrey started violently, for the utterly pleasant voice of the fantastic Boke was in the room.

"Your brother has a chance," said Boke's honeyed tones.

Sidney Lorrey, wrenching at the ropes which held him, gritted, "Get a doctor for him, damn you! Let me treat him! I'm a doctor!"

"Medical attention will not save him," Boke stated pleasantly. "But information will."

In an effort to see just which one of the men was Boke, Sidney Lorrey peered about intently. He could detect no betraying lip movements. He decided Boke must be in an adjoining room. There was an unnatural quality in the voice.

"Doc Savage has a remarkable institution in upstate New York for curing criminals," Boke said amiably. "The bronze man has discovered a treatment for the particular gland which is responsible for criminal behavior. Your brother, here, was in charge of the institution."

"How did you learn all of this?" Sidney Lorrey demanded. "It is supposed to be known only to Doc Savage and his five men and to those immediately connected with the institution."

"I had heard that criminals who went against this Doc Savage disappeared mysteriously and were never heard from again in their former haunts," said Boke's pleasant voice. "I became curious. This Doc Savage, it is a well known fact, does not take human life. What then, did he do with his prisoners. That was the puzzle. So I hired many investigators, and spent much money, and, eventually, I learned."

"What do you want with me?" Sidney Lorrey asked.

"One of the investigators whom I hired, a gentleman named Janko Sultman, double-crossed me," said Boke, ignoring the question. "But we will not go into that. Sultman is being taken care of."

"What do you want with me?" demanded Sidney Lorrey.

"I want the names of the men at Doc Savage's criminal-curing 'college' in upstate New York," said Boke. "I mean, the names of the surgeons who do the work there."

"I do not have that information," snapped Sidney Lorrey.

Boke's pleasant voice made bubbling laughter. "A lie, of course. You have visited the 'college' frequently. You have even conducted experiments there, using the facilities of the 'college' laboratory."

"I will tell you nothing," Sidney Lorrey said grimly.

The black-haired Leo straightened, sighed, and looked around as if irked by the waiting.

"Go to work on him, Leo," said Boke's voice.

Leo swung over easily and kicked Sidney Lorrey's face lightly and rapidly until scarlet began to ooze. Lorrey moaned, tried to scream, but they stuffed old cloth into his mouth.

Boke's voice, now filled with a ring of genuine horror, said, "I cannot bear violence, gentlemen! You will excuse me until you have secured the names of the surgeons in Doc Savage's establishment."

Sidney Lorrey, his interest in the mysterious Boke greater than his own agony, listened intently for some sound of a man leaving the other room, but there was no such noise.

Leo grinned lopsidedly and stroked his black hair back. "Funny guy, Boke," he said. "He's the biggest crook in the world, but if he had to do the dirty work himself, he couldn't pick a pocket."

"I can't make him out," some one said. "He ain't a coward. He claims his inner nature rebels at the thought of actually committing a crime. What a laugh!"

"I guess his crime gland ain't just right," Leo chuckled.

Leo now stripped off his coat, his evil face grim. He gave a low order and some one went out, evidently to an automobile parked somewhere near, for the fellow came back bearing a pair of pliers of the inexpensive type ordinarily included in tool kits.

Leo leaned over Sidney Lorrey, but jerked a hand at the divan near by on which lay the form of Robert Lorrey. One of the men went over and nudged the form. The figure shifted slightly and there was a groan.

"Your brother," Leo reminded Sidney Lorrey. "He will die if you do not tell us what we want to know."

"Why do you want the names of these surgeons?" Sidney Lorrey demanded.

Leo ignored that. "Are you going to give the information?"

Sidney Lorrey gritted, "I am not!"

Leo began plucking Sidney Lorrey's finger nails off with the pliers.

The human mentality is almost an incorporeity; it is a

thing productive of so many contradictions, so many mysteries, that it is not even fully understood by the psychologists who make the study of the mind their specialty. Students of the mind dispute each other when they try to explain, for instance, why one small boy may twist a cat's tail to hear it squawl while another lad may be horrified by the cruelty of such an act.

But the fact remains that some mentalities gloat over torture; and to some of these, the sight of physical pain, the joy of inflicting it themselves, acts as a wine, making them drunk with a sort of infernal ecstasy.

Leo's eyes became brighter, he breathed more rapidly, a grease of perspiration stood out on his forehead and he ceased to brush back the loose lock of black hair.

At first, he demanded of Sidney Lorrey the name of the physicians at Doc Savage's "college," putting the demands after each act of torture, but before long, he ceased doing that and went ahead in silence that was broken only by the awful sounds of the tortured man and the harsh grating of Leo's own breathing.

When the floor became slippery with crimson, Leo ordered bed coverings brought from another room, and Sidney Lorrey was rolled upon these. Lorrey was barely conscious now. Frightful things had been done to him, things that would mutilate him for life, and the other onlookers, hardened criminals, were becoming nauseated and turning away.

"He ain't gonna talk," one muttered. "Why not put him out of his misery?"

Leo, purple-faced, hot-eyed and intent, seemed not to hear, for he was engaged in the process of whittling Lorrey's fingers down to the bone, one at a time, and showing Lorrey, with fiendish chuckles, the naked gray of the exposed bones.

It was then that something began to happen to Leo, that his eyes started protruding. He dropped his knife, clasped his face and began to moan, then to shriek. His cries were hideous guttering bleats of pain and agony; his head tilted far back, then came forward and he bent almost double; he was gnashing his lips to shreds.

He fell over, convulsing, on the floor beside Sidney Lorrey, his eyes now all but out of their sockets; and after one final twitch, he relaxed completely and stopped breathing.

Sidney Lorrey, it suddenly developed, was far less gone than it had appeared. He must have been working slyly with his bonds, for now he jerked and got one hand free. He dived that hand into the clothing of the man who had just fallen a victim to the fantastic pop-eyed death. The hand reappeared with Leo's gun.

Sidney Lorrey held the weapon in the palsied clutch of both hands and croaked, "Stand still!"

None of the men moved. They marveled that Lorrey still lived, and they watched, fascinated at the gruesome efforts of the man to free himself of the rest of the cords and get to his feet. He was too weak to stand erect. He did not moan or otherwise voice pain as he crawled toward the divan on which lay the form of his brother.

The men in the room shivered and turned pale as Sidney Lorrey neared the divan; their eyes sought the door, but none dared flee. They were scared, terrified beyond reason by the fantastic fate which had overtaken Leo, and by the grim animation in the broken man-thing on the floor.

Sidney Lorrey took hold of the form on the divan. He shook it. He clutched blindly at the bandage on the forehead, so that it was pulled aside, showing the bullet hole in dead Robert Lorrey's head.

Sidney Lorrey screamed once, horribly, then he reared up and looked behind the divan. There was a man lying prone back there, too scared to move. It was he who had moved the body and groaned, so as to make Sidney Lorrey think his brother still lived, that they might use the brother's safety as a club to make Sidney talk.

Hoarse, uncanny sounds came from Sidney Lorrey's lips as he sagged back to the floor, and his eyes were wide and glazed. Red fluid from a cut on his forehead seeped down and pooled in one eye, but the orb did not blink. It glared, horrible and bloody.

It seemed that he was going to empty the gun which he held. He crawled toward the men, leaving crimson smears on the floor. His course brought him close to Leo's grotesquely sprawled body, and he peered vacantly at the protruding eyes.

Suddenly the vacancy went from Sidney Lorrey's stare. The madness still remained. And with it was a frenzied triumph, a mad, unreasoning mirth which caused him to cackle grotesque laughter.

"Look at him!" he screamed, and pointed at Leo.

None of the men looked. They had looked too much already, and it had put ice in their vitals.

"Look at your friend!" Sidney Lorrey shrieked madly.

"Look at the eyes! Look, and see how you are all going to die!"

Somebody croaked, "He's nuts!"

That was what they all thought, for Sidney Lorrey had been tortured enough to kill an ordinary man, and the hideous trick played with the body of his dead brother was enough to upset a more than ordinarily stable mind.

Sidney Lorrey was crawling toward the door, covering his retreat with the menace of his gun. The door he was making for was the one which led into the room from which Boke, the mysterious man with the voice of joy, had spoken.

"You want to know what is making their eyes stick out?" he gibbered hollowly.

No one answered, but that did not mean they did not want to know.

"It is the work of the Crime Annihilist!" Lorrey snarled. "Yes, call it the Crime Annihilist!"

He paused in the door, said, "You!" and jabbed a hand at the nearest man. "And you, and you, and you!" He jabbed at the others, then covered them all with an inclusive sweep. "All of you are destined to die! All of the criminals in the world will die!"

"He's nuts," muttered one of the listeners.

"Nuts!" Sidney Lorrey shrilled. "Insanity! Madness! It is a pleasure compared to what is to befall you."

Lorrey drew himself up dramatically and pointed at the pop-eyed body of Leo, yelling, "Look at him closely!"

No one looked.

"The work of the Crime Annihilist!" Lorrey shrieked.

Then Sidney Lorrey backed through the door into a room. He looked around vacantly for the weird Boke, but saw only three men with protruding eyes dead on the floor—Janko Sultman's men; but Sidney Lorrey did not know that, nor did he seem greatly interested, for he went down the rear stairway and out of the house.

He moved with an infinite slowness, leaving splotches of crimson, and should have been an easy victim; but the men he left behind did not follow him, for they were too horrified by what had happened.

A taxi driver whom Sidney Lorrey hailed thought his passenger was crazy, possibly with reason, and tried to take him to Bellevue Hospital. But Lorrey made threats and finally got out of the machine, and the hack driver fled, glad to get away with his life. After that, the snow-streaked cold of the Fall night swallowed Sidney Lorrey.

Chapter XI

TERROR OVER THE CITY

Monk, the homely chemist, beat his chest with hairy fists and bellowed, "They're the curse of humanity! They're parasites! They've caused half the wars of the world and they should all be shot!"

Pat, very trim and bronze-haired, came in from the outer corridor with a newspaper under her arm, and asked, "Who?"

Ham, the dapper lawyer, was carefully dipping the tip of his sword cane in a sticky paste which reposed in the back of his watch, in a special compartment which he had unscrewed. He glanced up.

"Lawyers in general," he smiled. "Monk is expressing an opinion."

"One lawyer in particular," Monk scowled, and glared at the sartorially perfect Ham.

"What set this off?" Pat demanded.

"That shyster," Monk indicated Ham, "done my hog a dirty trick! He put itching powder on Habeas."

Ham stood up suddenly and yelled, "I'm getting tired of having that accident in the pig race pull my topcoat down on the floor and make a bed out of it every chance he gets."

"So you put itching powder on the coat," Monk glared.

"And you got the stuff on you when you tried to find out what was wrong," Ham smirked.

Monk grimaced and scratched his furry wrist.

"Where is Habeas now?" Pat asked.

"In Renny's bathtub, soaking the stuff off," Monk admitted.

Pat snapped open the newspaper which she had brought.

"The press has gone wild," she said. "Look."

Black headlines were a foot deep across the front page. The mysterious pop-eyed malady was rampant, said the sheets, with more than a dozen persons dead during the night.

Half a dozen men had been found dead in a shabby rooming house, all of them known criminals, and a known murderer had dropped dead at the Association of Physical Health.

Nor were these all. In other parts of the city, men had been found dead with their eyes protuberant.

New York was scared, said the headlines. The trains out of the city were crowded. Workers were applying for winter vacations, and two or three persons, according to information amassed during the night, were thinking of closing up shop until the malady was past, or until some one found out what was causing the deaths. A tabloid predicted that this would be general.

The journalists pointed out again that, while some of the men who had died during the night undoubtedly knew each other, and one group was probably a member of a criminal gang, the majority of the victims had no possible connection with each other. This, the scribes seemed to think, could mean nothing but the presence of some fabulous epidemic.

That the hideous disease might strike anywhere, and in fact, was doing so, was played up.

Certain Southern health resorts had taken advantage of the scare to run advertisements suggesting that a visit to their establishments would be an excellent way to avoid the whole thing.

Monk scowled. "Those papers are making it worse," he said. "They should play it down. They're getting the whole town excited. They're scaring people. If this keeps up, it's liable to shut the whole place down. And poor people who can't afford it are going to get worried and spend their money and lose their jobs leaving town."

"Maybe they had best leave," Ham said grimly. "We don't know but that every life in the city may be in danger. It begins to look like this thing strikes everywhere."

Pat ran slim fingers through her hair and murmured, "Doc, do you think all of these pop-eyed deaths have a connection with Sultman and Boke and their schemes, whatever they are?"

Instead of answering, the bronze man said slowly, "I wonder what has become of Renny and the two Lorreys?"

Doc Savage's question remained unanswered during the next half hour. They waited in comparative idleness; the bronze man had put out every possible line in an effort to get in touch with the Lorreys, so there was nothing to do but kill time until something happened. Renny, too, should he have a chance, would be certain to call the apartment in an effort to locate Doc Savage.

Pat went out again when newsboys were heard yelling on the streets far below. She came back wildly excited.

"Look!" she screamed, and flourished a paper.

The headlines were as big as the page would hold, and the story which followed was in type which made it stand out in shrieking prominence.

DOC SAVAGE WANTED

POLICE NET OUT FOR BRONZE MYSTERY MAN

Police Inspector Clarence "Hardboiled" Humbolt tonight announced that he had twice received tips that Clark Savage, Jr., who has become famous as Doc Savage, the man of bronze, is responsible for the fantastic and horrible pop-eyed deaths. Each tip led to the discovery of a group of men who had perished from the mysterious pop-eyed death. Each tip was given by a pleasant voice over the telephone.

Doc Savage, Inspector Humbolt stated to reporters, was at one time under arrest, but escaped by employing one of the scientific devices for which he is famous. A general alarm has been spread for the bronze man.

The second telephone tip led to a house in upper Manhattan, where several men were found dead. Among them was a body identified as that of Robert Lorrey. He had been shot through the brain.

The story continued, giving details of the yarn, as well as the address of the house where Robert Lorrey and the other dead had been discovered. Doc Savage and his party read it through.

"A pleasant voice over the telephone gave the tips," Ham said grimly. "That means Boke."

Monk eyed Doc. "What about this?"

"We will go up there and look around," Doc said quietly.

"The police will have an eye open for us," Monk reminded.

Doc nodded. "For that reason, you three will stay here for the time being."

Monk did not look as if he thought much of the idea.

"What's the use?" he countered. "The cops will learn that Renny lives here, and they'll come around to invesigate."

The bronze man answered that by moving to the bathroom. The tub was full of steaming water, and in this stood the pig, Habeas Corpus. Doc lifted the shoat out of the water, then pulled the plug and let the tub drain, after which he reached up and turned the shower head so that it pointed straight up.

The tub promptly lifted on some mechanical support and

swiveled, exposing an expanse of masonry which was perforated with a slit large enough to permit the passage of a man. Metal ladder rungs led downward.

"Renny prepared this for a getaway," Doc explained. "It leads to a secret elevator in what is apparently a solid column of masonry. No one else in the building knows of it."

"Where does it come out?" Monk demanded.

"Nearly a block distant, in a private garage rented by Renny under an assumed name," the bronze man explained. "If the police come, you simply leave by this route, and they will never know you have been here."

"Swell," Monk grinned, and got down on his hands and knees to see how the mechanism operated. Satisfied, he straightened, looked around as if to say something, then blinked his small eyes.

Doc Savage was gone from the apartment.

Some moments later, a taxicab driver, huddled at the wheel of his machine, got the start of his life when a voice addressed him from the supposedly empty rear compartment.

"Drive north until I tell you to turn," the voice directed.

The hackman screwed his head around, but the light in the rear of his car had been turned out and he could make out only a shadowy bulk where his passenger sat. The driver rubbed his ears as he let out the clutch, wondering why he had not heard the door open or close.

He drove rapidly, slowing only when there was danger of skidding in the sheets of icy snow particles, and traversed nearly fifty blocks.

"Left here," advised the voice in the rear; and after they had gone two blocks: "Now, north."

The driver turned again to try to examine his fare, but once more the darkness thwarted him, and a moment later, he was too interested in something happening down the street ahead of him to think about his passenger.

The street was a long, gloomy one, lined by only a few houses. At the next block, a group of policemen stood in the street, stopping all cars, opening the doors and peering inside.

With a prickling sensation along the back of his neck, the driver of the cab pushed ahead. He halted when one of the officers flagged him with a hand.

"Got a fare?" the policeman demanded.

"Sure," said the driver.

An officer opened the cab door, looked inside, then pulled back and snarled, "What're you tryin' to do, wise guy? Kid us?"

The driver wheeled and his eyes flew wide, for the rear seat was empty.

"Uh-huh!" he stuttered.

"Get the heck outa here!" snapped a cop. "And take a tip and lay off the funny stuff."

The hackman went on willingly. Within the next four blocks, he noted a piece of paper blowing about in the seat beside him, and he picked it up. He grinned widely and pocketed the fragment of paper.

It was a ten-dollar bill.

Police Inspector Clarence "Hardboiled" Humbolt was bothered, angry, and taking no chances. He had made an examination of the house where Robert Lorrey had been found shot to death and the other men lay lifeless from the strange affliction of the protruding eyes. The medical examiner had come and gone. Finger-print men had done their work. The police photographers had taken pictures.

Hardboiled himself was in the lower hallway, talking to newspaper men. He had taken off his canvas shoes and was rubbing his feet gently, grimacing as if the rubbing pained him rather pleasantly.

The house was flat-topped, and flanked on either side by vacant lots which were surrounded by high board fences. There was a policeman in each vacant lot and two in the alley.

Hardboiled Humbolt held a small metal disk up for the newspaper reporters to examine. The disk was affixed to a linkage of small chain.

"Robert Lorrey wore this around his ankle," Hardboiled growled. "It is an identification disk with a number and an inscription requesting that Doc Savage be called."

"Did you call Doc Savage?" a reporter asked.

Hardboiled stopped rubbing his foot and swore. "If I knew where that bronze guy was, I'd call on him!"

"What does the disk mean?" asked another journalist.

"It means that the dead man was connected with Doc Savage," snapped Hardboiled. "He is the second fellow wearing one of those to be killed in the last few hours."

"Do you accuse Doc Savage of the killings?" questioned a cub.

"I don't accuse anybody," said Hardboiled, who knew what a clever lawyer could do with a libel suit. "I have evidence enough to warrant the bronze man's arrest."

Another reporter, the dean of the lot, said, "I do not think my paper will print any of these innuendos cast in the direction of Doc Savage. For one thing, Savage has the reputation of being straight as a string and of fighting criminals and of helping those who are in trouble. Furthermore, he is a man who has made incalculable contributions to surgical knowledge, and I personally know of charities and hospitals which he keeps in operation."

"All of which may be a build-up by Savage to make himself a big shot, while he's actually a master criminal of some kind," growled Hardboiled.

"Rats!" said the reporter.

Hardboiled Humbolt scowled and got up. He mounted the stairs, and because he did not put his tennis shoes on, and walked lightly so as to favor his bunions, he made almost no noise. Reaching one of the upstairs rooms, which was dark, he glanced inside. For once, he forgot his sore feet.

The chamber was a bedroom, and there was a mirror door on the closet. On this mirror, words were glowing in an eerie, electric blue. The big, well-rounded letters were perfectly decipherable from where Hardboiled stood. They read:

SIDNEY LORREY KNOWS CRIME
ANNIHILIST SECRET

Hardboiled Humbolt was so shocked that he made several inarticulate croaking noises. He had gone over the room personally a bit earlier and had found no such writing as this.

Thinking he caught a slight sound, he cocked an ear. Then he stepped in the room, wrenching out his gun.

"Stand still, you!" he grated.

There was no answer. Cold air brushed his face, and hard snow tinkled on window glass. Hardboiled felt for the light switch and got the bulbs white.

The room was empty, the one window was wide open—and the writing had vanished.

Hardboiled's angry howl brought policemen and newspaper reporters slamming up the stairs. They found the tenderfooted inspector leaning out of the window.

"Who left this open?" he roared.

No one seemed to know. To the reporters, Hardboiled told what had happened.

"This writing will come on when I turn the lights off," he said confidently. "It's phosphorous or something."

He stepped back and clicked the light bulb black. Then he looked at the mirror. He swore.

No writing had appeared.

Hardboiled tried it twice again without causing writing to appear on the mirror, then he went over, and with the lights on, used a pocket magnifier borrowed from a finger-print man. He found nothing, much to his amazement. They tried finger-print powder, and that brought out nothing.

"I can't understand it," the burly officer rumbled.

"The real original handwriting on the wall!" snorted a journalist.

Chapter XII

DEATH ON THE RIVER

It was well past midnight. The air was colder. The wind had become stronger. The gale howled around the cornices outside Renny's apartment like a lonesome dog.

Ham, the dapper lawyer, waved his sword cane and shrieked, "You awful mistake of nature! You missing link! You fuzzy ape! I'll chop you down to the shape of a human being!"

Monk, homely and simian, sprawled in a chair across the office, his eyes practically closed, his big mouth barely open.

The pig, Habeas Corpus, sat in the middle of the room and to all appearances, said, "The human race is made up of very funny animals. Even funnier than some others are certain small, sissified fellows who doll themselves up in flashy clothes and carry canes. Now you take—"

Ham suddenly seized a book and hurled it at the pig. Habeas dodged with a skill that had come from much practice, moved to the other side of the room and began again.

"Now you take—"

Ham roared, "I'm in no mood to listen to one of those funny hog lectures!" and glared at Monk.

Monk pretended to be asleep.

Pat Savage, occupying a chair in the background, tried to keep a sober expression on her attractive features. Monk and Ham quarreled during all their time together, each going to extreme and sometimes childish measures to aggravate the other.

Monk's present performance was one he could depend upon to throw Ham into a rage. Monk had gone to great pains to learn ventriloquism for the specific purpose of throwing his voice to Habeas and having the shoat express choice opinions of Ham, who was touchy on the subject of pork in general, anyway.

Monk, throwing his voice, made Habeas seem to say, "This funny human race is marked by the presence of parasites. A parasite is a fellow everybody else could get along very well without. An example of a parasite is a lawyer——"

Monk stooped and sat up suddenly as Doc Savage came in.

"Find Renny?" Monk demanded.

The bronze man said, "I managed to get into the house where Robert Lorrey was killed. Use of the ultra-violet lantern showed a message in Renny's handwriting, on a mirror door."

"Then Renny had been there!" Ham said grimly.

"What did the message say?" Pat put in.

" 'Sidney Lorrey knows Crime Annihilist secret,' " Doc Savage stated. "That was the message."

Monk scratched in the rusty bristles which stood out straight on the back of his neck.

"Crime Annihilist?" he pondered aloud. "Who's he?"

Ham flourished his sword cane suddenly. "Jove! I believe an annihilist would be one who destroys. And hasn't it occurred to you that the victims of this pop-eyed death have been criminals?"

"Not all of them, shyster," Monk reminded. "That last newspaper we read said two had died who were not crooks. One was a Park Avenue sport and the other a banker."

Ham frowned, changed the subject completely, and asked, "Doc, did you see our friend Hardboiled Humbolt?"

"The gentleman walked in on me while Renny's message was fluorescing under the ultra-violet lantern," said the bronze man dryly. "A convenient window allowed me to get away before he realized just what it was all about."

Pat put in sharply: "If Sidney Lorrey knows the secret of what is behind all these hideous killings, suppose we find him."

"An excellent idea," Doc agreed. "We will try Sidney Lorrey's laboratory on the barge."

Because the night was unnaturally cold for the season, and the waters of the East River proportionately warmer, there was a thick gray suds of fog over the water. The gale swept this upon the shore, where it froze and deposited thick white frost, giving the terrain a ghostly, Arctic aspect.

Sidney Lorrey's barge was like a great white box, with

another and smaller white box placed in its middle, and the whole set in a steaming cauldron. But because it was very dark, the boxes did not look so intensely white.

There was a great silence, broken only by the gale and the sound of tug whistles audible at long intervals. Close to the river, the noise of the waves could be heard.

For a long time there had been no sign of life, but now the macabre aspect of the cold scene was broken. A figure moved, shifting from the shelter of a piling head to the lee of a great, unused timber. There was great furtiveness in the marauder's manner.

The skulker was bundled in a black overcoat, the velvet collar upturned; there was a muffler of black silk, thinly marked with white, wrapped around the lower face. The hat was light gray, blending with the snow, and concealing the remainder of the wearer's features.

This strange individual, who obviously did not wish to be seen, seemed to be watching Sidney Lorrey's barge. From time to time, his head lifted over the timber while eyes examined the barge.

The steam off the river and the windborne snow, combined to mask the barge, and from where the mysterious figure lay, not overly much could be seen. The skulker evidently concluded to crawl closer. He wormed along for a few yards, then shifted over and got behind another timber and crawled along that.

But he did not crawl far. A hand—a great, corded hand of bronze—abruptly drifted over from the opposite side of the timber and clamped down on the crawling one's neck. The marauder emitted one stifled bleat of surprise and pain. Then he was wrenched bodily over the timber. He struggled a bit, but could accomplish but little against the metallic giant who held him.

There was a stir in the near-by murk, and Monk, Ham and Pat scuttled forward. They joined Doc Savage and his captive.

"Who is he, Doc?" Monk breathed. "Sidney Lorrey?"

Ham said softly, "It's lucky you spotted this fellow, Doc. Otherwise, we'd have walked right onto the barge without ever knowing he was around."

Doc Savage, saying nothing, pulled the silk muffler down and shoved the prisoner's hat back, disclosing his features.

The man was middle-aged. He had fine features, ruddied a bit by the cold, and a cropped blond mustache, blue eyes and very even white teeth.

Monk leaned close and held a big fist under the man's

nose. The man recoiled nervously. Monk demanded, "Who are you?"

"Oh, my!" he gasped. "I knew I was making a mistake in acting on my own initiative."

His voice was mild, his words rather too prim for the circumstances.

"Who are you?" Monk repeated.

"Doctor Mortimer Basenstein," the other admitted.

Monk looked as if he did not believe it. "What are you doing here?"

The other squirmed, moistened his lips, looked as if he would rather not answer.

Monk held his fist up like a bludgeon. "Spill it!"

"I am a practicing physician," said Doctor Mortimer Basenstein. "About two hours ago a man came to me for treatment. He was horribly beaten, cut and mutilated. I think he was slightly insane. He raved about being the Crime Annihilist who was going to kill a million criminals. He was quite mad. He said the Crime Annihilist was going to kill all of the crooks in the world."

"What name did this man who said he was the Crime Annihilist give you?" Doc Savage asked sharply.

"Sidney Lorrey," muttered Basenstein.

Monk grunted something explosive, for he had not expected this word that Sidney Lorrey was the mysterious Crime Annihilist who caused men to drop over with their eyes protruding.

Ham leaned forward with his sword cane and tapped the point of their captive's chest.

"You have not explained just what you are doing here," he pointed out.

Basenstein shuddered. "I am a kind-hearted man, and I have a respect for my profession," he said. "This Sidney Lorrey proved to me that he himself is a licensed physician."

"True," said Doc Savage.

"Then you know him?" Basenstein looked up.

The bronze man nodded.

Monk, his manner still hard, said, "What are you doing here?"

"I followed Sidney Lorrey," Basenstein explained. "The man is temporarily demented, I tell you, and I wanted to help him. If I turned him over to the police, no telling what would happen. I tell you, this Lorrey claims he has killed scores of criminals already."

Monk gave a terse opinion of the story. "Pretty thin."

Basenstein snapped, "I tell you, I am a physician with an office several blocks from here on Seventieth Street."

Doc Savage glanced at Ham and spoke a few words in the ancient Mayan dialect. Ham nodded and moved away, the darkness swallowing him.

It was fully five minutes before Ham came back and stated, "There is a Doctor Mortimer Basenstein who has an office on Seventieth."

"I told you," declared Basenstein.

Doc Savage asked, "Where is Sidney Lorrey now?"

Basenstein pointed at the barge. "On that."

"We will find him," the bronze man stated, and moved forward.

Some distance away, a man lay prone on a pile of timbers with a pair of binoculars clamped to his eyes. The glasses had an extraordinarily wide field, which made them effective as night glasses. The man had a handkerchief tied over his lower face, perhaps to keep his breath from fogging the glasses, and again, perhaps to hide his features.

He eased backward, using every caution to keep from making a noise or displaying his person too prominently. A moment later, he joined several other men. They, like himself, all wore dark overcoats which kept them from standing out too prominently in the murk. They were careful to keep away from snow backgrounds.

"It worked," said the man who had been using the binoculars.

"He's goin' with Doc Savage?" asked another.

"Sure!" said the first.

That seemed to be what they had awaited, for they all crept back away from the vicinity of the river front, as if not wanting to take chances of being discovered.

Doc Savage, nearing the gangplank which led to the old barge that Sidney Lorrey had converted into a laboratory, held up an arm and the others stopped, permitting him to go on ahead.

Basenstein asked softly, "Who is that man?"

"Doc Savage," Monk advised.

"Oh!" said Basenstein. "The man of mystery!"

Doc Savage advanced toward the gangplank, started across it, halted suddenly and his strange flake-gold eyes roved. He brought out the flashlight which operated from a spring generator rather than a battery and raced the thin beam back and forth.

Then he removed his coat, balled it and flung it hard. There was a mound of snow at the end of the gangplank, between its end and the side of the barge deck house. The coat knocked the snow aside a bit, disclosing the body of a man.

Doc Savage advanced carefully, spraying the flashlight on the snow before him. Reaching the body, he turned it over.

The dead man was stocky, clad in evening clothes, and his round, full face was oily even in death. His eyes were gruesomely protuberant.

Doc Savage straightened, and the snow, swept along the barge deck by the terrific force of the wind, covered the form again almost as if a sheet were being drawn over it.

The bronze man went to the deckhouse door, but did not open it. He listened. There was no sound. He stood aside as a matter of habitual precaution, and knocked.

There was a loud concussion inside the deck house. A tuft of splinters jumped out of the door. The rifle bullet which had made the hole moaned toward Monk and the others, but passed slightly over their heads.

Mortimer Basenstein, terrified by the proximity of the bullet, emitted a screech of terror. Monk snorted angrily and clapped a hand over his mouth. They struggled. Basenstein seemed gripped with a mortal terror.

A drumming from the shore drew all eyes. Monk released Basenstein and snatched under his arm for his supermachine pistol. Figures became distinguishable in the room.

"Cops?" Monk growled questioningly.

"No," said Ham.

Red sparks jumped from the approaching forms and gun sound slammed noisily.

Pat Savage was carrying a larger hand bag, and she wrenched it open and drew out an enormous single-action six-shooter. It had been her father's gun, and she had practiced with the weapon until she had the proficiency of an old-time Western gun fighter.

She shot from the hip, not pulling the trigger, for there was no trigger on the gun, it being stripped down for fanning. She simply rocked the hammer back with a thumb and let it fall. The concussion as the antique went off was terrific.

One of the attackers started dancing around crazily, fell down on the snowcovered ground and threshed and kicked and finally became still.

"*Tsk, tsk!*" Monk clucked. "Such bloodthirstiness!" He took a careful aim with his supermachine pistol.

"Mercy bullet," said Pat. "Doc made some up special for this cannon."

Monk's superfirer emitted its bullfiddle moan. Three of the approaching men folded down magically. Startled, the rest flopped flat and were lost in the nodular masses of timbers, old machinery, piles of hawser and other appurtenances common to wharves.

One of the assailants threw a grenade. No one but Doc saw it coming, and the bronze man knocked the others flat so that the grenade, exploding near by, did nothing but deafen them.

"Back on the barge," advised the bronze man.

They retreated, using all the caution possible, keeping down. Monk fired his supermachine pistol once more. Ham used his twice. So far as they could tell they hit no one, but they kept their foes down.

The high rail around the barge furnished shelter against anything but a high-powered rifle bullet.

Monk, turning over to stare at the windows in the barge deck house, growled, "Didn't somebody shoot at you from inside, Doc?"

"A bullet came through the door," the bronze man admitted.

"Then we'd better get out of sight of those windows," Monk pointed out. "Who d'you reckon fired it?"

Ham answered that. "Sidney Lorrey, of course!"

Bullets, striking the barge rail, had the sound of heavy hammer blows, and where they topped the rail they dug out splinters and split the planks of the deck house.

Basenstein was moaning over and over, "I hate violence! I cannot stand it! They are trying to kill us!"

"Shut up!" Monk advised.

Another grenade made a great uproar and threw pieces of metal from some rusted machinery alongside which it exploded.

"A young war," Monk growled, trying to find a target for his supermachine pistol. "The cops will hear this and come running."

Doc Savage worked back, and the others followed him. They rounded a corner of the deck house, where they were more perfectly sheltered.

Beside a dark window, Ham stood erect, hesitated, then peered inside. He could make out nothing. He tried the sash—and to his surprise, it opened. He shoved it up.

A voice inside the barge said wildly, "Stay out of here! Stay out of here!"

"Sidney Lorrey's voice!" rapped Ham. "I've heard the man speak. He was visiting his brother at our upstate place once."

"Stay out!" shrilled the voice in the barge.

It was made hollow by the acoustic tricks of the barge interior, but the words were clearly distinguishable.

"Damn you!" shrieked Sidney Lorrey's voice. "I won't let you get hold of me again!"

Ham yelled, "Don't be a sap, Lorrey. This is Ham. Doc Savage is here!"

His answer was as phenomenal as if a firecracker had exploded in his face.

The roof came off the deck house and rode upward on a sheet of flame, disintegrating as it arose. Some of the deck house wall folded outward; the sides of the barge split; the whole craft heeled, and gory red flame jumped from every door, window and crevice.

Ham, knocked backward by the concussion, would have gone overboard had it not been for Doc, who seized his leg and kept him on deck. The others, lying prone at the moment, were merely bounced about by the explosion.

Upstream, as the tide now flowed, there was a flash and a great blaze of light. There must have been an explosion, too, but their eardrums, already punished by the blast on the barge, failed to register it as more than a *pf-f-f-t!* of a noise.

The gasoline barge had been split apart and set afire. Gasoline was spreading over the water, carried down by the slow ebb tide and moving toward Sidney Lorrey's barge.

"We'd better vamoose," Monk gulped. "There's gonna be a real bonfire here in a minute!"

The attackers on shore seemed as stunned as any one by the sudden pyrotechnics. They were on their feet, some staring, some retreating. Perhaps the sound of police sirens in the distance had something to do with their withdrawal.

Ham fired his supermachine pistol at the men, but the dapper lawyer was still dizzy from the shock of explosion, and he missed. Some one shot back with an automatic until the gun was empty. Then the attackers began to flee in a body.

Monk waved an arm at the burning barge. "What about Sidney Lorrey?" he asked.

"Go on," Doc told him. "I'll look around."

Monk nodded; with Ham and Pat he moved off the barge, then all stopped and waited for Doc Savage. They could see the bronze man working through the wreckage, endeavoring to inspect the barge interior.

But the explosion had started a great fire. In addition, the burning gasoline was piling up around the barge, the flames mounting, setting the planking afire. The heat was terrific, already melting snow a score of yards back from the river.

Doc Savage moved swiftly, venturing into what seemed like solid sheets of flames, and Basenstein moaned, "He will be burned!"

There was another, lesser explosion forward in the barge. Fire had gotten to a fuel tank, throwing sheets of flaming petroleum. Smoke mounting from the pyre was streaked with green and yellow and white, undoubtedly coming from burning chemicals.

"These chemical fires are bad!" Monk yelled. "Better get out of there, Doc!"

The bronze man was already moving away from the blaze. A great leap took him to the shore, and he joined the others. They ran away from the spot, using caution, half expecting their late assailants to rush them.

They were out of sight before police cars whined up, followed by ambulances, then a hook and ladder, hose carts, and a general emergency wagon.

Doc Savage, watching, noted that the police failed to discover the gunmen who had driven Doc and his party aboard the barge.

"I wonder what outfit them cookies belonged to?" Monk pondered aloud, referring to the gunmen. "D'you reckon they drove us onto the barge, knowing it would blow up?"

"Unlikely," Doc Savage told him.

"How d'you figure, Doc?"

The bronze man did not answer. He seemed not to have heard the inquiry.

Basenstein, pale and trembling, asked, "Did you find Sidney Lorrey?"

"The fire," Doc told him, "spread too quickly."

"Then Sidney Lorrey is dead!" Ham said slowly.

"And that means the finish of the Crime Annihilist," Monk echoed.

Chapter XIII

ULTIMATUM

Monk was wrong. In spite of what had happened to the unfortunate Sidney Lorrey, the uncanny menace of the Crime Annihilist still existed. They learned that when they reached Renny's apartment.

Doctor Mortimer Basenstein went to the apartment with them. While they were still leaving the vicinity of the burning barge laboratory, he had said, "I am sure those gunmen saw my face. I am worried. Suppose they should try to take my life?"

"Why should they?" Ham countered.

"I shall feel safer with you gentlemen," said the other.

And Doc Savage agreed to that with a nod, somewhat to the surprise of Monk, Ham and Pat.

The telephone was ringing when they entered Renny's apartment, after crossing the city furtively, so as not to be sighted by the police. Doc Savage answered the instrument. Monk crowded to his side, hoping it was Renny calling.

But the voice was one so utterly pleasant to hear that it caused Monk to clench his fists and show his teeth in a snarl that would have done credit to a Congo ape.

"Boke!" he gritted.

"This, I trust, is the estimable Doc Savage?" Boke inquired pleasantly.

"What do you want?" Doc asked emotionlessly.

"To explain the affair at the barge a few moments ago," Boke replied over the wire. "In case you may be in doubt, it was my men who attacked you. They had made a previous attempt to board the barge, and one of them, ah—met a misfortune."

"I found his body," Doc admitted.

"No doubt," Boke agreed. "I sent more of my men to get Lorrey, and they seem to have had the bad luck to arrive when you and your party were there."

"Why?" Doc questioned. "Did you want Sidney Lorrey?"

"He is the Crime Annihilist," said Boke.

Doc asked, "What do you want with me?"

"We want you to find Sidney Lorrey and commit him to a madhouse where he belongs," said Boke.

"Sidney Lorrey's voice spoke to us an instant before the explosion on the barge," Doc Savage stated quietly. "After the blast, I attempted to get his body out, but the fire was too furious to get near the spot from which his voice had come."

Boke screamed, *"What?"*

That single wild exclamation of astonishment told Doc Savage and the others more about the mysterious Boke than all they had learned prior to that moment, for the ejaculation was in a different tone, and the alteration showed that Boke had been speaking in a disguised voice. The deliciously pleasant tone was not his normal manner of speech.

"What?" Boke repeated. "You mean that Sidney Lorrey—is dead?"

Doc Savage half turned; Monk was on another telephone, endeavoring frantically to have the call traced.

"Is that all you wanted with me?" the bronze man inquired.

"Wait!" Boke gasped hurriedly. "You have got to find the Crime Annihilist. *He just killed another of my men!*"

"Why?" Doc made his voice disinterested. "In some respects, this Crime Annihilist is doing a service to humanity."

Boke said, "Wait; I wish you to hear some one," and there was a brief pause, and a scuffle, a thump as if a chair had been upset, along with a few labored curses.

Over the wire came Renny's great, booming tone.

"Don't do a damn thing these guys want you to, Doc!" Renny rumbled. "As soon as they get this Crime Annihilist out of the way, they're going ahead with their original plan to seize one of the specialists from your upstate——"

There were blows, more grunts, a squeal of some one in pain, then Boke resumed speaking.

"Your man seems never to get enough fighting," he said dryly. "But you heard him. You know we have him. His safety is the price for your services. Find this Crime Annihilist, get him in an insane asylum or in a jail, and we will release this man Renny."

"On the other hand, the Crime Annihilist, who seems to have mastered a mysterious method of killing criminals, will get you if I leave him alone," Doc said. "Then Renny will be free to walk out."

"Renny will not walk out from where we are putting him," Boke promised. "He will die without ever being found, if anything happens to us."

Doc Savage began, "Just what connection does my upstate institution have with——"

Boke said, "Think my proposal over," and hung up.

Monk slammed his own telephone down, waved his long arms and yelled, "That dumb telephone operator! She kept insisting the wire you were talking on was out of order."

Doc picked up the telephone over which Boke's call had come, listened, and got only emptiness.

"It is out of order," he said briskly. "Sounds as if it had been cut."

"Tapped!" Ham yelled. "Somewhere between here and the telephone exchange."

"We'll make an examination," Doc rapped, and swung out of the apartment. At the door, he told Pat, "You stay here with Basenstein."

Monk and Ham followed Doc. The telephone circuit, they knew, entered a master conduit which extended down through the tall apartment house to the basement, where it connected with the regular conduits.

Basenstein seemed nervous after Doc and the other two had gone. He kneaded his fingers together, picked at splinters which his clothing had acquired during the action on the barge.

"Do you think there is any danger?" he asked Pat.

"Sure," Pat said unkindly. "We all have an excellent chance of being killed."

Basenstein put a wry twist on his lips that was meant for a smile. "You are quite a remarkable young woman."

"Fooey!" said Pat. "I wonder if Renny keeps anything to eat in this place."

She wandered off in the direction of the modernistic kitchen, but it was significant that she kept her enormous single-action six-shooter in hand instead of replacing it in the bag.

A peculiar change jerked over Basenstein the instant Pat was out of sight. He whipped a pencil and a notebook from his pocket and wrote rapidly. Then he searched for something with which to weight the missive. A silver half dollar served the purpose, and he snapped a rubber band around this.

As silently as possible, he made his way to the window. Thanks to the efficiency of modern construction, it opened with a minimum of noise. Basenstein leaned out.

The street was a cold, bleak expanse far below, warmed but little by street lights and the lenses of parked taxicabs.

Basenstein threw his message wrapped in the silver half dollar, then followed it with his eyes and looked relieved when he saw it was going to land near the middle of the street.

A man detached himself from the shadows of a building across the street, scuttled hurriedly, and picked up the message. He faded back into the murk.

Basenstein put the window down quietly.

Behind him, Pat said, "You after fresh air or something?"

Basenstein proved himself a consummate actor. He pretended that he had just reached the window, and he raised it high.

"I am wondering if I can see Doc Savage below," he said, and thrust his head out, making a show of glancing about. Then he closed the window and said, "No sign of him."

"I put the percolator on," Pat advised. "This thing may go on for days and days before anybody gets any sleep. There is stuff for sandwiches in the kitchen."

Doc Savage, Monk and Ham came in from the outer corridor, catching Pat's eye, made an empty-handed gesture.

"Wire was tapped in the basement," he advised. "Bird had flown. Nobody see, nobody hear. Out of luck."

Pat eyed Doc. "What are we going to do?"

The bronze man, addressing them all, advised, "You will stay here until I return or communicate with you."

Monk asked pessimistically, "And if we don't hear from you, where do we start looking for you?"

"At headquarters," Doc advised.

Monk exploded. "But the police are watching——"

Doc Savage said, "It is essential to use the headquarters laboratory for certain experiments." Then he went out.

Down on the street, it was not as dark, but the wind was stronger and there was more snow in the air. It was not snow falling from the thin clouds, but hard flakes scooped up by the gale and whirled about with great violence.

Doc Savage selected a taxicab parked in a dark spot and entered it, as he had done in another case earlier that night, before the driver saw his face. He reached up and switched off the dome light, then directed the driver downtown.

The hackman was too cold to show interest in his fare, but he did say, "I'd turn on the radio, boss, but the static is a fright to-night. Got worse the last couple of hours. Guess it's this blizzard."

"Never mind," Doc told him.

At a street intersection where a traffic light went red, they pulled up alongside a police car. Doc rolled down the cab window and heard the police short-wave set spewing noisy volumes of static. One of the two officers in the car was working with the radio dial and cursing.

The cop looked up hastily, then scowled at the radio, for he was hearing a sudden, weird trilling sound of fantastic, unreal notes. It was an exotic thing, this trilling, something that might have been a product of the cold night gale—or a caprice of the radio.

The trilling died, and the officer did not associate it with the presence of the taxicab, which had now gone on.

Three uniformed officers were on duty in the lobby of the skyscraper which housed Doc Savage's headquarters. The bronze man saw them as the taxicab drifted past in a whirl of snow.

He got out of the machine two blocks beyond, walked a block to the right, then two blocks north and swung into a side street which ran along the rear of the skyscraper.

It was doubtful if the police had learned of the basement garage which the bronze man maintained in the big building. Not even the building employees themselves, for the most part, knew of its existence.

Doc Savage let himself into the garage with its array of motor vehicles, which ranged from a large, innocent-looking moving van which was armored like a tank, to a shabby, ramshackle coupé which might possibly make a hundred and fifty miles an hour on a straightaway but which looked like a twenty-dollar job off a second-hand lot. A narrow concrete corridor led the bronze man to a special high-speed elevator which in turn let him out on the eighty-sixth floor.

The corridor was empty. The door of his headquarters was unprepossessing, bearing in small bronze letters the inscription:

CLARK SAVAGE, Jr.

Two of the three rooms inside were enormous; with the smaller reception room and office, they took in the entire floor of the titanic structure. Reception room and library, Doc Savage ignored. He entered the laboratory.

The bronze man went to work in the labyrinth of apparatus, setting up electrical coils, tubes, connecting an audio amplifier of tremendous sensitivity and power. Most of the devices with which he tinkered would have been understood by an electrical engineer; but there were a few so complex, so unusual of design, that even an expert on such things would have been baffled.

This laboratory held many things to be found nowhere else, or perhaps at only one other spot—a strange, remote retreat to which this strange bronze man retired periodically to study and experiment, shut off from the world so completely that none knew where to find him or how to get a message to him.

Only Doc Savage himself knew of this other spot—of its location, rather. Monk, Ham and the rest of his aides knew of its existence, knew he called it his Fortress of Solitude. But that was all they knew. The bronze man would simply disappear—for days, weeks, maybe months—and none would know his whereabouts.

Then he would come back as mysteriously as he had gone, and usually with him came some new discovery in the field of electricity, chemistry, surgery, or another of the sciences at which he was skilled.

One thing Monk and the others did agree upon: These protracted periods of concentration, away from every outside influence, were responsible for the bronze man's fabulous knowledge.

Outside the skyscraper laboratory, the wind whooped and howled. Inside, there was frequent noise. Always, these noises possessed a sameness, coming from loud-speakers which Doc Savage had hooked to his apparatus.

The sounds were akin to the crackle, mutter and crash of ordinary radio static.

The minute hand on the chronometer crawled around and around. The bronze man's wrist watch kept with it almost to the second, where it lay after he had removed it and placed it aside to get it out of the magnetic fields of the apparatus with which he was working.

Outside, the wind suddenly stopped dead. Clouds went out of the sky. The sun came up with what seemed like suddenness.

The telephone rang.

Boke's utterly pleasant voice said, "This, I trust, is the estimable Doc Savage?"

The bronze man reached swiftly to a button, pressed it. The bell which that button rang was an imperative order to the telephone operator to trace the call.

But Boke was canny. He spoke with great speed. "Call Renny's apartment," he rapped.

Then he hung up.

A moment later the operator was reporting, "I am very sorry, but there was no time to trace that call."

Doc Savage said nothing, but dialed the number of Renny's apartment.

He got no answer.

The door of Renny's apartment was closed, but a loud voice penetrated through it. The speaker was in a howling rage.

"Of all the low-down, infernal tricks!" the voice squawled. "I'll tear your legs off! I'll feed you that sword cane."

"Quit bellowing, you missing link!" snapped Ham's milder voice. "Try to get loose."

"I'll haunt you!" Monk bawled. "I'll get in your hair and take it all out by the roots!"

Ham yelled, "It's too damn bad they didn't take you instead of the hog!"

Basenstein's voice said nervously, "Gentlemen! Gentlemen! Please stop it!"

Doc Savage, his appearance showing no signs of the terrific rapidity with which he had come from his downtown head-quarters to the apartment, came in from the corridor and stood looking at the tableau in Renny's modernistic living room.

Monk, Ham and Basenstein were arrayed on the floor, tied with stout manila rope. Not only were their wrists and ankles bound securely, but they were roped together in a chain so that the more they struggled, the tighter their bonds became. It was an expert job of tying.

Doc Savage went to work swiftly, asking no questions. His fingers showed their incredible strength in the speed with which the knots opened.

Ham, freed ahead of Monk, retreated uneasily from the glaring chemist.

"You shyster!" Monk bawled. "You'd better take a running start or they'll be scraping you off the walls!"

Ham, for once looking a bit concerned in front of Monk's rage, began, "Listen, Monk, when I told them how much you thought of Habeas Corpus, I didn't think——"

Monk's roar drowned him out.

"What happened?" Doc demanded.

"That fashion plate!" Monk glared in Ham's direction. "Half a dozen lugs came charging in. They took us by surprise. Ham told 'em I thought more of Habeas than I did of my right eye. So they took the hog."

The instant Monk's ropes were loosened, he tore them off and heaved erect. His rusty hair bristled. He showed all of his teeth. And he charged Ham purposefully.

Basenstein moaned and covered his eyes in the manner of a man who expects to see murder done.

But Monk never touched Ham. The gorillalike chemist came to a stop. He rocked back on his heels foolishly. Then he grabbed at his head.

"Ouch!" he squawled. "My head!"

A hideous thing was happening to Monk's eyes. They were slowly protruding. He groaned in agony, sank down on the floor and held his head with both hands.

Doc Savage seized Monk, spread him out on the floor. He got smelling salts from a medicine cabinet and hot black coffee which bubbled on the kitchen stove, and administered both to Monk.

The homely chemist sat up after a time, his eyes normal again. He looked about foolishly.

"That pop-eyed business!" he exploded. "It got hold of me! Hell! I ain't no crook!"

Ham suddenly threw back his head and screamed. He sank down on the floor, rolled over and over, hands clamped over his chest. After a moment the others, who had been startled, realized he was gripped with paroxysms of laughter.

"I always knew," he gulped, "that the missing link was a crook at heart."

Monk got up suddenly, glaring, fists clenched. Then he looked extremely pained, his eyes seemed about to pop, and he sat down and held his head.

"Damn the luck!" he groaned. "Whenever I think of giving that shyster what he's got coming, I get that goofy feeling."

Ham went off into fresh mirth.

"Where's Pat?" Doc Savage asked.

Ham stopped laughing as if he had been slapped. He seemed to think deeply, to realize how he had been laughing, and he looked slightly sick.

"They took her," he said, and his voice was hoarse, low.

"Who did?" Doc demanded.

"Those men who came in here with guns and tied us up," Ham elaborated. "They were Boke's men."

Basenstein pointed at the table and said, "They left a note for you, Mr. Savage."

Doc went to the table. The note was not in an envelope. He held it up—a plain, white typewritten sheet, folded once.

"It's Renny's paper and they used Renny's typewriter," Ham said grimly. "They wrote it out while they were here, and the typist wore gloves."

Doc Savage read his own name, then went on through the body of the typewritten missive:

> We are entertaining your attractive cousin, Pat Savage. She will be kept with your other friend, Renny. The two of them will be released when you have disposed of this mysterious Crime Annihilist.
>
> We could, of course, have taken Monk and Ham. But you will need assistance in finding this Crime Annihilist, so we left them to help you.
>
> BOKE (By an agent)
>
> P.S. The pig goes in the bargain.

Basenstein said, "They were quite cold-blooded and efficient."

"On the contrary," Ham said, "they were scared stiff. They were worried. They fear this Crime Annihilist."

Basenstein murmured, "I thought that——"

"You haven't seen as many crooks as I have," Ham told him. "These babies were worried."

Monk tapped his own chest. "I maintain this Crime Annihilist business is a phony. It affects guys who ain't crooks."

Ham snorted unkindly. "If you're trying to prove that by your own case—the evidence is not convincing."

Doc Savage said, "We are leaving New York City immediately."

Basenstein jumped violently. "But why?"

The bronze man went over and switched on a radio masked in a modernistic cabinet. He did not tune in a station, but set the dials on an empty frequency. The set began to spew and crackle.

"Blazes!" muttered Monk. "Such static!"

"Growing worse by the hour," Doc said quietly.

Ham, comprehending, nearly dropped his sword cane. "You mean that this—this static has something to do with the Crime Annihilist?"

The bronze man nodded. "Exactly. The experiments in the laboratory proved it conclusively."

"You say we are leaving the city," Basenstein murmured. "Where are we going."

"That," Doc told him, "will have to remain unknown to you. We will go by plane, and you will be blindfolded."

Basenstein simply spread his hands in baffled agreement.

"We will eat now," Doc said. "It may be some time before we get another chance."

Chapter XIV

BOKE DECIDES

Doc Savage, Monk and Ham moved into the kitchenette where Renny, who was a skilled cook as well as a great engineer, kept a store of food which he prepared himself on occasion.

"I am not hungry," Basenstein said miserably, and sat down in a chair.

"You will be when you smell the grub," Monk told him.

Basenstein remained in the front room, looking very downcast. But the moment the other three men were out of sight, he produced his pencil and paper furtively and began to write. He scribbled briefly and in great haste. His efforts to find more silver coins to weight this missive were futile, so with an animated grimace of regret, he contributed his watch to the purpose.

As before, he got the window up silently, took a careful aim and hurled his message. Then he carefully shut the window.

The wind had died completely; in the chill morning calm, the note fell with scarcely a flutter, landing in the street. Basenstein winced as it hit, for the watch had been an expensive one.

A man, bundled to the eyes in topcoat and muffler, ran out into the street, scooped up the note and the wreck that had been the watch, and retreated. He did not glance upward or otherwise behave suspiciously.

The man had been waiting inside an apartment house doorway, but he did not return to that spot. Instead, he walked down the street, not too rapidly, and turned the first corner. He seemed to be searching for a taxicab. There was only one machine parked near by, and he entered it.

"Drive north," he directed.

The hackman put his vehicle into motion, and as he did so, he reached down to a secluded spot under the seat and grasped a small wire which had a ring in the end. He pulled this out and held it several moments.

In the rear of the hack, the passenger was reading the message which Basenstein had thrown from the window of

Renny's apartment. He made a clucking sound of surprise as he noted the contents:

Savage has Crime Annihilist secret and is leaving the city for mysterious purpose.

The reader absently put a hand over his mouth and coughed. He coughed again, more violently, then seemed to strangle slightly. Suddenly his eyes flew wide and he wrenched at the door handle.

"Lemme out of this damned thing!" he yelled.

The driver grinned wolfishly, but the faintness of the passenger's words showed that the cab body was as nearly soundproof as it could be made. The fare was still wrenching at the door handle, but the door, mysteriously locked, would not open. The passenger's struggles became weaker. He still gagged and coughed and beat his chest.

In a few moments, he sagged down on the floorboards and his spasmodic kicking subsided.

The cab driver turned into a side street, reached around and opened the cab door easily from the outside. He drove for a few moments to let the gas, which had overcome the fare, be swept out by the inrush of fresh air. Then the chauffeur felt under the seat to make certain the gas container trip valve, operated by pulling the concealed wire, was closed.

Stopping the machine, the driver got out. He felt the wrist of the man in the rear. There was a strong pulse.

The driver appropriated the message. Then he hauled the unconscious passenger out, dumped him on the sidewalk, got back behind the wheel and drove off rapidly.

The taxi driver turned west, ignored two shivering citizens who tried to flag him down, and crossed Central Park on one of the express lanes which were sunken below the sidewalks, bridle paths and boulevards. He pulled to the curb before a brownstone house in the Fifties, got out and entered a door which was dropped three steps below the sidewalk level. The door was barred heavily on the inside, and a thick-shouldered man stood behind it.

"Something for the boss," said the driver.

The man at the door lifted one thick shoulder toward the upper regions, but said nothing. The driver mounted a narrow stairway. It was dark in the house, the air was warm and smelled of mimosa.

The message carrier came to a door, shoved through, and

grinned sourly at the muzzles of several pistols which were trained in his direction.

"What's the idea of not knockin'?" somebody snarled.

"Nuts to you!" said the driver, and went to a door, opened it and admitted himself into the kitchen. There was a dumbwaiter shaft, and he opened the door of this.

"Boke!" he called into the shaft.

It was a brief moment before the utterly pleasant voice of Boke demanded, "Well, what is it?"

"This phony Basenstein threw a note out of Doc Savage's window," said the driver. "I glommed onto it."

"Send it up," Boke requested.

Complying with the order, the driver reached into the shaft, grasped the ropes and ran the dumbwaiter down. He weighted the note in place, using a heavy pistol cartridge for the purpose, and ran the platform back up. Then he listened. A moment later, he grinned.

Up above, wherever he lurked, the mysterious Boke was cursing heartily, and there was little laughter in his voice.

"What fools we are!" Boke swore expressively. "The whole thing is perfectly clear!"

"You mean you know who the Crime Annihilist is?" the driver demanded.

"Of course!" said Boke.

"Who is he?"

"This note you just delivered gave it away," said Boke. "See if you cannot figure it out. In the meantime, wait down there. Tell the doorman that we shall have callers shortly. He is to admit them when they give the password, 'Desperate Measures.' "

"What are these guys gonna be?"

"Do not worry about that," said Boke. "You will be able to recognize most of them."

That terminated the conversation, and the driver left the dumbwaiter shaft.

At the top of the shaft, the room from which Boke had spoken was dark, the curtains being drawn tightly, and additional heavy draperies spread out to shut off every vestige of outside light. The figure of Boke himself was completely lost in the black void.

The door of the room was opened and Boke stepped out. He crossed a hallway and entered a room in which Patricia Savage, Renny and Janko Sultman were bound and gagged. The pig, Habeas Corpus, was tethered in a corner by a chain.

Renny eyed Boke intently. The big-fisted engineer was

seeking to pick out details about the man's appearance which would later serve to identify him. He was seeing as much of Boke as he had ever seen.

For Boke wore a long topcoat—a grotesquely long topcoat which was like a robe and covered even his shoes. Above that, a muffler was tied. Colored glasses and a hat so huge that it sat down over Boke's ears topped off the disguise.

Boke presented a ridiculous figure. He was a laughable apparition. But the disguise was effective.

He stood over Janko Sultman and looked at the latter's upstanding, frizzled hair. Sultman's small mustache was pulled out of shape by the gag which distended his jaws.

"You are a clever rascal," Boke stated reluctantly, and laughter and pleasantness was once more in his voice. "Even if you did try to double-cross me."

Janko Sultman made inarticulate sounds around his gag.

"I hired you to investigate this 'college' which Doc Savage maintains in upstate New York," Boke continued. "The way you did it shows you are clever. I need clever men now. Therefore, I think I shall give you another chance."

Sultman croaked more vehemently at this.

Boke bent down, untied Sultman and removed the gag, then straightened swiftly and stepped back, hands buried in the topcoat pockets, where bulges indicated the presence of guns.

"Come," Boke directed. "We will have a conference downstairs."

Pat and Renny glared as Boke and Sultman left the room.

Sultman stumbled as he moved, for he was stiff from being tied. It was some moments before he spoke.

"What about Lizzie?" he demanded.

"Lizzie?" Boke laughed dryly, hollowly. "During the night, Lizzie passed away with his eyes protruding."

"You mean he's dead?" Sultman gulped.

"Exactly!" Boke agreed. "He was a victim of the Crime Annihilist."

Sultman was introduced into the presence of the men in the room downstairs. These looked him over so viciously that Sultman, frightened, slunk into a corner, seated himself and said absolutely nothing.

Boke now retired to another room. Taking up a telephone, he proceeded to make numerous calls. At all times he used a disguised voice. The name of Boke did not seem unknown to the individuals he called, and when the pleasant voice requested their presence, at a conference aimed at their own good, most of them agreed. A few, though, did refuse suspiciously. But Boke seemed to think his average was very good.

Outside, the city streets were beginning to fill, although the hour was unnaturally early. It was especially notable that many of the pedestrians carried traveling bags, and were headed in the direction of railway stations.

Fear was on almost every face. Women were nervous, and here and there, one was hysterical. The people bought newspapers, read them and became grim and pale. More than one individual started for his office, got as far as the nearest newsstand, bought a paper, then read it and went back and packed his baggage.

The headlines were unbelievable. The story was the most fantastic within the memory of many.

Almost fifty persons had died in New York City during the previous night. The eyes of all had protruded.

Baffled physicians were now advocating that the city be evacuated, for nowhere else in America was any one dying with his eyes popping.

Boards of health in near-by cities, it was reported, were holding hasty sessions to decide if it would not be best to quarantine New Yorkers, in order that the pop-eyed malady might not spread.

A specialist had arrived from Chicago, and was as mystified as anybody as to the cause of the deaths.

An astronomer who was something of a publicity hound had declared he believed mysterious atomic streams were being shot to the earth from outer space, and were causing the strange deaths. His statements were given quite a play and his picture was prominent. He based his declaration on the unusual amount of static every one was hearing on their radios.

Indeed, the static was now so bad that the police radio cars were helpless to receive calls. Radio engineers were investigating the phenomenon, and most of them attributed it to the storm and to spots on the sun. The only fault with this theory was that the astronomical observers insisted there had been no unusual number of sun spots.

At mid-morning came the supreme surprise.

Extra editions brought the report.

All of the pop-eyed death victims were criminals!

John Henry Cowlton, the Park Avenue playboy who had been the first victim, had been discovered to be a clever society jewel thief with many robberies and at least one murder on his record.

Everett Buckett, the Wall Street wolf who was the second victim, was a leader in an enormous stock-swindling gang, and at least two persons they had swindled had been murdered to shut their mouths.

And so it went down the list. The police were now madly at work investigating records of the dead, and in most cases they were finding plenty to show that the corpse, in life, had been far from honest. Individuals who had been supposedly possessors of lily-white characters were being found to have been crooks. There were exceptions, but the police freely intimated they expected to find these were crooks, too.

Strangely enough, this did not quiet the citizens of New York. If anything, the horror increased. Not all of the dead crooks were persons who had committed heinous crimes. One man had been beating his wife when he fell dead with his eyes sticking out.

The newspapers became wilder, if possible. They freely predicted that something had happened to the world, starting in New York City, and that every dishonest man was going to die, no matter how small his offense against society.

It was surprising how many people began to remember little slips. It was surprising the frantic efforts they took to remedy them, too. The mission down on the Bowery reported an increase in converts. Unusual numbers of persons were observed entering churches.

Police stations began to receive nervous visitors who wished to confess crimes, thinking that might help. These first comers were usually petty offenders.

Then some great brain down at police headquarters got an idea. He promptly gave out an interview saying he was sure that these crooks who confessed their crimes were safe from the pop-eyed death.

The newspapers printed that, and the cops sat back to reap a heavy harvest of scared crooks.

Long before noon, however, the first of a series of sinister visitors arrived at the house now occupied by the mysterious Boke and his gang. This individual arrived in a large car, driven by a chauffeur, and his machine was preceded and followed by two other cars, in each of which rode four grim-looking bodyguards.

The escort cars parked up the street while the man in the limousine alighted and entered the house.

The doorman goggled at the visitor, recognizing him as one of the most famous barons of the "alky" racket during

Prohibition days. The big shot was now the king of the policy racket and considered to be many times a millionaire.

The czar of crime looked scared.

Shortly afterward, more visitors arrived. Without exception, they were gang leaders. They were not only crooks and killers, these men, they were gentry who had attained a point where they hired lesser thugs to do their dirty work. They were the overlords of crime.

It was a choice collection which finally gathered in the upstairs room. Fully three-fourths of the organized crime in New York City and environs was represented.

Boke appeared. He still wore his comedy character disguise of long overcoat and muffler and colored spectacles.

Some one growled at Boke that he was among friends and he'd better get out of his disguise if he knew what was good for him, but Boke told the speaker to go to hell, then began making a speech. So pleasant was Boke's voice that every one was held spellbound.

Boke recited the names of some of the victims of the past night's holocaust, names which were very well known to most of those present. Mention of the bankers, however, brought forth scowls, for these professional crooks considered their operations amateur competition.

"You will notice, gentlemen, that all of the unfortunate victims are men outside the law," said Boke.

"Nix!" said a fat crook. "The law ain't got a thing on me, but I had one of them spells anyhow. I damn near croaked."

Boke said patiently, "What I meant was that every one who has died was, to put it bluntly, a criminal. If you want to use nicer words, call them unsocial individuals."

"Something's poppin' off the damn crooks," said one fellow bluntly. "So what?"

"I think it is time we did something about it," Boke announced. "Otherwise we are all likely to die. Just how many of you men have had queer feelings in your heads during the night."

Considering that some of the crooks, out of pride, and maybe from force of habit, lied about it, it was evident that a large number of them had experienced seizures, or had men in their gangs who had had the spells.

Boke stated, "I want you to work with me and take my orders. An individual known as the Crime Annihilist is causing these deaths. He is out to rid the world of criminals. I am probably the only living man who knows who the Crime Annihilist is."

Boke said all of that very rapidly, so no one could get in

an objection before it was all out. Then he gave them time to think it over. Some of these big shots had gained their positions by shooting all competitors, and had brains which worked very slowly. So Boke gave them plenty of time.

Then Boke passed the note around:

Savage has Crime Annihilist secret and is leaving the city for mysterious purpose.

"That came from a very reliable source," said Boke.

The filched message came back to Boke; he then read it aloud, slowly and distinctly. Every one present had pretended to read the missive, but Boke knew that some of the big shots could not read a word, and he did not want to embarrass anybody.

"Doc Savage!" a poultry racketeer chief snarled. "I've been afraid of that guy for years, thinkin' he might get on my trail. But I never thought he'd pull anything like this!"

"It's Savage," another snapped emphatically. "The bronze guy is a mental wizard. He can do anything. He's thought up some way of wipin' out criminals wholesale."

Another man groaned, "Boys, let's all catch a steamer for Europe until this blows over."

"And give up my sweet pickin's!" jeered the man beside him. "Not much!"

"But supposing the Crime Annihilist is not Doc Savage?" said another man.

"Everything points to Savage as the Crime Annihilist," Boke told them. "At first, I suspected a man named Sidney Lorrey, but he—ah, went insane and killed himself by blowing up his laboratory on a barge."

"I read about that fire in the paper," said a voice.

"I have captured two of Doc Savage's very close friends," Boke said pleasantly. "One is his cousin, Patricia Savage. The other is the engineer, Renny. I have told Doc Savage to produce the Crime Annihilist, or the two prisoners will be killed."

The assembled masterminds of crime looked at Boke with a new interest.

"For the love of little dogs," one muttered. "You went up against that bronze guy and got away with it?"

"I did," Boke stated with some pride. "Furthermore, I have kept several jumps ahead of him."

"What do you advise doing?" a voice queried.

"Keep close track of Doc Savage," Boke announced.

"Then lead the bronze man into a trap, using my two prisoners as bait."

An evil-faced man in the back of the room yelled, "And then let me have 'im! I'll take care of 'im!" He drew a big automatic, waved it dramatically.

The gun arm gesticulated more and more violently, then the bloodthirsty man's other arm joined in waving, and he began to stagger around and make gargling noises. This persisted for some moments, while the others stared in horror. The victim fell down on the floor, kicked violently, rolled over on his back and became quiet.

His eyes were almost out of their sockets.

Chapter XV

UPSTATE

Doctor Mortimer Basenstein at the precise instant that the gang leader died in Boke's presence, was feeling desperately in his coat pocket for the book of blank papers on which he had been writing his notes. Basenstein was worried. He had laid his coat aside for a moment while he shaved, and the book of blanks had disappeared.

Basenstein walked nervously around the living room, looking behind modernistic divans and under chairs, but without locating his vanished property.

He went to a door and peered through, then stood there for a moment, fascinated.

Doc Savage was taking his exercises. Rather, he was just completing them.

Monk sat on a bed, and after a casual glance at Basenstein when he first appeared, continued to watch Doc and perspire. Monk always perspired when he watched Doc work out. Such was the power of suggestion provoked by the bronze man's strenuous routine.

For nearly two hours the bronze man had been working out, going through a ritual to which he had adhered with daily regularity since childhood. He had already finished the muscle-building part of the exercises, which were similar to the ordinary physical culture movements, although more strenuous.

A portable case contained other and more unusual appurtenances to the exercise routine. These consisted of a device which emitted sound waves above and below the audible range, careful use of which had, in the course of years, given the bronze man an almost super-sensitive hearing.

There was a collection of phials holding various odors, and the bronze man identified these repeatedly to make more delicate his sense of smell. He read pages of Braille printing, the system of upraised dots designed for the blind, to sharpen his sense of touch. And there were other devices, more complex, which he had designed himself.

The bronze man's giant frame showed little evidence of fatigue, although he had not slept during the night.

Basenstein went back and continued his hunt for his notebook, but with no greater luck than before. A few moments later, Doc Savage entered the room and strolled casually toward the window.

He bent suddenly, moved a corner of a small rug, then straightened. He held the missing book of blank sheets.

"This yours?" he asked Basenstein.

Basenstein made a pretense of feeling of his pocket, then smiled. "Why, yes, I believe it is. It must have dropped out of my pocket."

Basenstein took the pad of blanks and masked a relieved sigh as he pocketed them. There had been nothing written on them, so no harm was done. But he needed those blanks for future secret messages.

A bit later, Doc Savage joined Monk in the bedroom. Ham was not present in the apartment.

"He smell a rat?" Monk asked softly.

"No," Doc replied. "I believe he thought he actually had dropped the book of blanks."

Monk now slipped from a pocket the uppermost sheet which had lately adhered to Basenstein's pad of blank paper.

The sheet had been treated in a manner familiar to police experts—by the use of chemicals. As a result, the tracings of messages which had been written atop it were discernible as faint lines. Fortunately, they had not been written one exactly atop the other, so it was not difficult to read them.

The first stated:

Doc Savage got orders to find Crime Annihilist on pain of having Renny killed.

The second was the missive which had eventually found its way under the eyes of the mysterious Boke.

"This Basenstein is a phony," Monk growled. "He's a spy."

"Obviously," Doc agreed.

Monk got up. "I'm gonna bump 'im around a little and start him talking."

"Wait," Doc said. "We will let him play along with us."

The homely Monk squinted at the bronze man. "You don't very often have an idea that sounds as nutty as that."

Unperturbed, Doc said, "We may find use for this Basenstein."

The telephone rang. It was Ham.

"All set," he advised.

Two hours later, Doc Savage was maneuvering a tri-motored speed plane through the bumpy air over the mountainous upstate section of New York. The clouds were low and thick, and the air surprisingly warm, for a sudden thaw—warm winds out of the south—had followed the storm.

Snow still remained on the hilltops, but it was melting rapidly and sheets of water covered the bottoms of draws, the small meadows; streams were writhing torrents of muddy water.

Ham occupied the cockpit with the bronze man. Ham looked very unlike his usual self, his face being darker and his hair possessing a reddish color. This was part of the disguise Ham had donned in order to assemble equipment without being molested by the police. The job had fallen on Ham because he possessed a physical appearance less striking than that of Doc Savage or the gorillalike Monk.

Monk came forward, leaned close and growled, "That mug Basenstein is at it again."

"What now?" Doc asked.

"He's writing notes," Monk advised. "Whenever we pass over a town, he drops one out."

"I had noticed that," Doc admitted.

Monk blinked his small eyes. "Well, ain't we gonna do anything about it? This guy will get to thinking he's good after while."

"Let him alone," Doc said. "He may prove very useful."

Grumbling under his breath, Monk retreated to the rear of the cabin.

Ham asked curiously, "When did you first get wise to this Basenstein?"

"When he joined us at Sidney Lorrey's barge laboratory," Doc replied.

"Good night!" Ham exploded. "How?"

"Remember that I looked around the vicinity of the barge when we came near it?" Doc asked.

"Yes." Ham nodded. "And you found Basenstein skulking."

"I also found several men waiting in the background," Doc said. "They were wondering if Basenstein would succeed in deceiving us."

Ham exploded. "And you let Boke think his agent, this Basenstein, had taken us in from the first! What was the———"

Monk yelled, "Thar she blows!"

The terrain below had become wilder, more rugged. A single road, a trail, barely discernible in the murky afternoon light, progressed through the timber, following creeks and tiny valleys for the most part. The road ended at a massive metal gate.

From the gate, a high, stout wire fence ran in a circle which enclosed many acres. This fence, woven, surmounted with barbed strands, was fully fifteen feet high.

From the air, it looked as if the fence enclosed only a small lake and a log building which might have been a hunting lodge. On one side of the lake, shoving its bald mass up to a considerable prominence, was a hill which seemed to be of solid, gray stone.

There was nothing else inside the fence—just the lodge, the lake and the bleak stone hill.

But back from the gate, perhaps a mile, surmounting a hill of its own, was a small, unpretentious cabin.

Doc Savage studied that cabin at great length through the binoculars.

Then he sent the plane down over the fenced enclosure and circled the lodge near the gate.

A man came out of the lodge, which was situated near the gate. He wore rough woods garments and might have been a caretaker. He looked up at the plane.

Doc Savage turned the controls over to Monk, leaned from the cabin window and made semaphore signals with his arms.

Below, the man on the ground laid himself flat on his back so that his own semaphored reply might be more distinguishable. His arms jerked to various angles.

Ham, going back in the plane cabin, chose the moment of the signaling to stumble and fall headlong onto Basenstein, with the result that their passenger, if he could read the semaphore signals, missed out on them.

Doc Savage drew back and said, "Everything is quiet."

Then he resumed the controls and sent the plane away from the strange enclosure, strange because there was no good reason why any one should want to fence off so thoroughly a piece of ground in this wilderness.

The plane was an amphibian, and the bronze man cracked the landing wheels up so that the floats were clear for a descent on water.

"Blazes!" Monk whispered. "Aren't we gonna land at the 'college'?"

"And give the secret away to Basenstein?" Doc countered.

"We could pitch him overboard," Monk suggested hopefully.

"No," Doc replied. "Basenstein is serving a very useful purpose. He may save us a great deal of trouble."

Monk sighed. "Blasted if I get this."

The plane swept over another small lake. Doc tilted the craft down, pinched the throttles and changed the propeller pitch. Wing flaps made automatic adjustment for their decreased speed. They settled on the lake surface without undue commotion or shock.

The water was murky with mud, and when Doc cut the three motors, they could hear the gurgle and roar of freshets emptying into the lake. There was still snow under the larger trees, but it was fast melting. The ground was all but covered with a film of water. Even the air seemed saturated.

"A swell time for camping out," Monk complained.

"Stay in the plane," Doc advised. "It will be more comfortable."

But Monk and Ham both spilled out in the shallow water and waded ashore with the bronze man, leaving Basenstein behind in the plane.

"Listen, Doc," Monk said hopefully. "How about giving us the lowdown?"

"Yes," Ham put in. "Just what is behind this seemingly pointless trip up here?"

"The Crime Annihilist and his work," the bronze man said slowly. "Unless my guess is wrong, we will find the whole solution near here."

Then the bronze man moved away, seemingly without haste, and stepped behind a clump of small evergreens. Monk and Ham waited for him to reappear, became suddenly suspicious, and ran to the thicket.

The bronze man was gone.

"Dang it!" Monk complained, and endeavored to follow Doc's trail. He lost it within a few yards.

"You might as well give it up, you hairy mistake," Ham advised. "Doc suspects some one, but has no proof; so he will not express an opinion."

They stood there, snapping at each other quarrelsomely. It

occurred to neither to glance back toward the plane, which was at the moment shut off from their view by brush.

In the plane cabin, Basenstein was furtively busy. The big aircraft was fitted with radio transmitting-and-receiving apparatus, and Basenstein was crouched before the instrument panel. The set was a strange one, and he showed by the facility with which he got it in operation that he was not unfamiliar with radio apparatus.

He raised the wavelength adjustment slightly, then cut the microphone into circuit and spoke rapidly.

"Basenstein reporting," he repeated over and over. "Basenstein reporting."

"Report," directed a voice over the receiver.

"Doc Savage landed plane on lake," Basenstein stated into the transmitter, then gave a surprisingly accurate description of the lake's whereabouts.

"Excellent!" said the operator of the other radio. "Any further information on who the Crime Annihilist is?"

Basenstein hesitated. "I have been thinking," he said at last. "Doc Savage is acting very strangely about this affair. I think his own men are puzzled. It may be that Doc Savage is actually the Crime Annihilist."

"I think that myself," said the distant one.

Basenstein declared, "It is dangerous for me to talk;" then he severed the radio connection.

He carefully returned the dials to the setting at which he had found them, and lifted his head to see if he had been observed. He could see no one. He thrust his head out of the cabin, and could hear Ham and Monk squabbling.

Monk and Ham, as they inevitably did when together for long, had gotten around to personalities and the matter of Habeas Corpus.

"You hairy freak!" Ham snapped. "That hog has been a pain to me from the beginning, and I hereby state that what has happened to him does not worry me at all."

Monk glared. He opened and shut his hairy hands.

"Maybe it doesn't now," he growled. "But it's going to later. Because if anything has happened to that hog, I'm gonna work out on that neck of yours!"

"Any time you're ready!" Ham invited, and flourished his sword cane meaningly.

Monk scowled and picked up a convenient limb. The bough was as thick as his arm, but the homely chemist handled it as a schoolmaster would a switch. He started for Ham purposefully.

Then he pulled up, dropped the limb, looked dazed, and grasped his head. His eyes popped the merest trifle.

"Blazes!" he gulped and sat down heavily. *"Ow-w-w! My head!"*

Ham said, "I should cut your throat and put you out of your misery," and smiled widely.

Monk glowered, tried to get up, then relaxed, grimacing as a fresh burst of pain seized him.

"What ails you?" Ham asked cheerfully.

"That Crime Annihilist funny feeling in my head, damn you!" Monk grated.

"You get it every time you try to jump me, don't you?" Ham asked hopefully.

"Yes, blast you," Monk admitted.

Ham's large orator's mouth stretched in a smile that threatened his ears. He leaned on his sword cane and began to speak in a gentle, unhurried tone.

There were many things which Ham had long wanted to tell Monk, but had not dared. Monk, with his apish strength, could whip half a dozen like Ham, and the dapper lawyer knew it. The knowledge had tied his tongue.

But now he unburdened himself. He went far back in the niches of his memory and dug up choice expletives, goading personalities and plain insults. He heaped them on Monk with an unholy joy. He became flushed and started perspiring, and his eyes turned bright and he stopped frequently for a good laugh.

Monk sat and took it. Several times, he got to his feet as if intent on slaughtering Ham, regardless of the consequences. But the terror of the mysterious Crime Annihilist's spell overtook him and forced him back. He finally stuffed a little finger in each ear.

Ham waxed more and more eloquent. The memory of all the past insults Monk had ladled out, all of the irritations Monk had wrought with the aid of his pet pig, his ventriloquism, came back to Ham's thoughts. They were legion. And Ham got verbal revenge for all of them.

The moment was to stick in Ham's memory as the biggest of his lifetime. He had long wanted to goad Monk to the limit when the hirsute chemist was in a position where he could not talk back.

But Ham's enjoyment came to a rough ending.

A plane, dropping down out of the sky with motors shut off, so that it made little noise, was almost overhead before it was noticed. Even then, Monk and Ham did not discover it.

A wild yell from Basenstein drew their attention to the yellow amphibian.

Men leaned out of the plane overhead. They held black, lumpish objects in their hands. While their craft was still some distance away, they began hurling the objects overboard. The things burst in the brush with *plopping* violence.

Ham, who had been addressing Monk as if the homely chemist were his bitterest living enemy, suddenly shed his animosity.

"I got a lot more to tell you!" he snapped. "I want you alive to hear it!"

Then he seized Monk, helped him erect, and tried to aid him in reaching cover. But the plane was too fast for them. Passing overhead, it left a rain of the black metal things which burst dully, and Monk and Ham suddenly felt the painful bite of tear gas in their eyes. They were almost instantly helpless.

Monk, banging trees and brush in an effort to flee the vicinity, yelled, "Dang you, Ham, if you hadn't been making so much noise, we would have heard that sky wagon!"

Ham said, "Shut up and run, you hairy accident!"

Over toward the lake, they could hear more of the big tear-gas bombs bursting. Basenstein was yelling something that they could not understand. Then the noise of the plane motor above decreased sharply; they caught the whine of air in flying wires, then the noisy rush of water as it landed on the little lake. Staccato bursts of the motor brought it closer.

Monk and Ham, knowing fully just how helpless they were, bent every effort to leaving the vicinity. But they heard men running behind them, men who came closer with a speed which proved that they were wearing protective masks.

Some one struck Monk heavily from behind. Then, strangely enough, the one who had struck the blow began to cry out in pain.

"You fools!" said the utterly pleasant voice of Boke. "Keep calm! Don't get excited. This Crime Annihilist thing only hits you when you're excited."

"Dot is true," called Janko Sultman's slightly foreign accent.

Hard things which could only be gun muzzles menaced Monk and Ham. They were roughed about, and being helpless, blinded as they were, had of necessity to surrender.

A triumphant gang of captors herded them back toward the planes, after handcuffs were linked on their wrists.

Monk, reaching the lake and being ordered to wade out to

the planes, fell down purposefully, so that the tear gas was washed from his eyes. This, and the fact that its effects were already wearing off, enabled him to see a little.

Staring at his captors, he identified Janko Sultman at once. Several other faces, familiar to him, puzzled him briefly, then he realized he had seen them in the newspapers. They were the faces of big-shot criminals.

Monk searched for Boke—and was disgusted when he discovered that the individual who must be Boke was effectively disguised by a flying suit and a muffler tied across his features.

"Where is Doc Savage?" Boke demanded.

Monk ignored that, and roved his eyes until he located Basenstein. The plump physician was standing to one side, but two of the plane arrivals were positioned close to him.

"You called this gang!" Monk yelled angrily.

"I did not!" Basenstein snapped.

One of the men beside Basenstein demanded of the physician, "Where is Doc Savage?"

"I don't know, you damned rascal," said Basenstein.

The questioner instantly launched a terrific blow with his fist. Basenstein staggered backward, splashed flat in the water, and his split lips, oozing crimson, reddened the cold lake about his face.

"You'll damned well talk!" yelled the man who had struck the blow. He seemed about to say more, but instead, seized his own head with both hands and moaned, "The Crime Annihilist!"

His eyes were protruding a little.

"Take the two planes," Boke directed calmly. "Everybody aboard."

Monk, eyes still streaming, peered wonderingly at Basenstein as he was lifted and flung into one of the planes. Monk was very puzzled. Basenstein did not seem to be a member of Boke's crew.

Almost together, the two planes took the air.

Chapter XVI

DOUBLE TRAP

Doc Savage was almost two miles away and traveling back toward the small lake with all the speed of which his trained sinews were capable when he heard the two planes take off. He had heard the strange aircraft approach the lake and had turned back.

The bronze man halted, stood listening long enough to realize that the two planes were headed in such a direction as to fly near where he stood, then he moved swiftly to one side, entering a clearing where he could signal the planes with some chance of being seen.

The tri-motored ship which Doc, Monk, Ham and Basenstein had flown into the woods country appeared almost at once. Doc gestured. The pilot apparently saw him immediately, for the big ship heeled around in the sky and came sliding toward him.

The bronze man watched the quality of the flying intently. It was a sloppy job; either Monk or Ham would handle the controls far more expertly. Warned that something was wrong, the bronze man retreated hastily.

Instantly, men popped heads and shoulders out of the plane cabin. They pointed rifles, revolvers, submachine guns and sawed-off shotguns. Tufts of woodland loam began to jump up around Doc. Then came the reports of the weapons, distinguishable over the sound of the planes.

The second plane heeled in. This pilot was more expert. He kept his craft near the stalling point, air speed at a minimum. And some one in the ship had a regulation aircraft machine gun, its ammo cans charged with tracers. Slugs ran down in a weaving gray string, chattered in the mud, splashed pools of melted snow, snipped twigs off the trees.

Doc Savage whipped from one scanty shelter to another. The trees here were not evergreens. Moreover, the surroundings had been burned off a few years ago, so that the trees which now grew were young, thin things offering almost no safety.

Below the clearing was a creek, a roaring torrent almost full from bank to bank with snow water, and Doc headed for that. There were overhangs which might furnish shelter visible along the rim of the stream.

Again and again the planes dived, raining lead. The bronze man dipped a hand inside his clothing, brought out a tiny chemical smoke bomb of his own concoction, and tossed it down beside him so that the blooming cloud of black smoke enveloped and hid him. He had used these smoke bombs to escape on other occasions.

But it did not work this time. Boke's men in the planes simply swooped low and emptied out nearly half a bushel of tear-gas bombs. Doc was driven on toward the creek.

Boke's plane dived again, every cabin window crowded with gunners. They were experts with weapons, these men; they had lived by them for years.

A delighted yell went up as Doc Savage caved down suddenly. The pilot banked hastily. They could see the bronze giant squirming on the ground, could make out a flood of crimson spreading over his shirt front.

"He's hit bad!" Boke shrilled.

Then they saw Doc drag out smoke bombs—one, two, three of them. He flung them to the right, left and ahead, so that a great cloud of black spread over where he lay.

The planes continued to dive and pour lead into the smoke, the roar of motors and the stutter and bang of guns mingling in a holocaust of sound.

A slight breeze, stirring through the soaked woods, pummeled the smoke, shoved it aside, pushed it out over the stream.

Boke cursed shrilly through the muffler that he wore over his face, for he had sighted a twisted form below, reposing under the scanty shelter of a tree.

"He crawled away in the smoke," Boke yelled. "There he is! Get him!"

The plane moaned down, jerked its nose up and screwed a tight bank. Guns clamored. Branches fell off the tree under which the form lay. Bark showered. Mud splashed. Water geysered.

The form itself jerked about as bullets pummeled it. Flying mud covered it until it was hardly distinguishable. Again and again, the planes dived and the attackers emptied gun magazines.

Then, triumphant as chicken hawks which had made a kill, the two craft spiraled in search of a landing place. The clearing where they had first sighted Doc Savage was too small to permit either ship to be set down. And there was no other opening of consequence near.

"No need of landing, anyway," Boke shouted pleasantly. "He's dead!"

Janko Sultman, plump and excited, scrambled to Boke's side and gripped the mastermind's arm.

"Der Crime Annihilist!" he bellowed. "It is not harm us! It is no more!"

Boke settled back in his seat. There was wild relief in his laugh.

"Right!" he yelled amiably over the motor roar. "Every time we became excited, or tried to kill, that infernal spell of the Crime Annihilist would strike. But this time it did not."

"How you explain dot?" Sultman pondered in a shout.

Boke waved an arm back at the creek bank where a bullet-torn, mud-splattered form lay under a ripped tree.

"The Crime Annihilist is dead," he said. "It may be that we will never know how he did it."

Sultman shook his head slowly. "Dot was a strange thing, dot Crime Annihilist thing."

Boke now went forward, spoke to his pilot, and the aviator began looking around for a clearing in the woods. Finding one, he set his plane down expertly enough, cut the motor, then turned in his seat to watch the other ship alight and taxi up alongside.

Every one got out, excepting an armed guard watching over Monk, Ham and Basenstein.

The big shots disported themselves like small boys at the dismissal hour on the last day of school. Their evil minds had been relieved of a burden and they showed it. The future looked rosy. They gathered around Boke.

"Let's get back to the big burg," one grinned.

"I'll throw a party to celebrate," said another. "It'll be a party to end all parties. Boy, I'll spend ten grand on it!"

"Where's the guy who wanted to go to Europe?" shouted a third delightedly. "Let's ride 'im on a rail."

"I move we make up a kitty for Boke!" yelled some one. "I'll put in ten grand to start the ball."

"And I move this guy Boke peel that muffler off his face so we can see who he is," bawled a voice.

Boke held up an arm, motioning for silence.

"Keep your money," he said. "You owe me plenty for showing you how to get rid of this Crime Annihilist. I want you to pay off by doing me a favor."

"Now what the hell?" somebody growled.

"Unmask him," suggested a tough voice. "I've heard of this baby Boke, and that's why I strung along with him. But now I want to see his map."

Boke took a small automatic from his clothing. "I have a very good reason for keeping my face hidden," he said. "If you could see my face, you would understand why."

They looked at the automatic, not knowing just how to take its threat. Some one asked, "Just what do you want us to do?"

"I want you to raid Doc Savage's criminal curing 'college' and force some of the surgeons there to divulge certain information," said Boke.

"College?" a beefy racketeer muttered. "What're you talkin' about, buddy?"

Boke began speaking. He told of the fact that criminals who became entangled with Doc Savage had, in the past, disappeared, and now this had made him suspicious. He had hired Janko Sultman, he explained, to investigate, and Sultman had, by months of painstaking investigation, learned that Doc Savage maintained a strange institution in upstate New York, where he made honest men of these crooks.

"We got hold of a minor attendant about the place and bribed him," Boke explained. "From him we learned that Doc Savage had discovered that crime is in a sense, a disease. In other words, there is a small gland in the human body the secretions of which have a great deal to do with whether a man is a satisfied citizen or a cold-blooded criminal with no sense of right and wrong."

"What's this all leadin' up to?" someone interrupted.

"Doc Savage treats this gland, making it function normally," said Boke. "Or rather, his surgeons at the institution do the treating."

Boke paused, in order that suspense might rivet the attention of his listeners upon his next words.

"These surgeons know how to treat this 'crime' gland so as to make a criminal, as well as cure him," he stated. "It is that secret I want—the knowledge of how to make criminals."

"Nuts!" growled a voice. "What's the idea? Where'll that put anything in your pocket?"

"You lack imagination," Boke chuckled. "It is my plan to seize bankers, industrial magnates, politicians, and administer them the drug which will make them criminals. They will not know what is being done. Later, myself or my agents will approach these men and enlist them in my unlawful enterprises. They will accept. Having access to thousands, even millions of dollars, they will, as criminals, appropriate those funds. I will make it my business to see that a share of the money gets into my hands."

"This," commented one of the big shots, "is the goofiest thing I ever heard of."

Boke said patiently, "I have thought it all out with great care. It will work. The men I make into criminals will not know exactly how crimes are committed, and they will be highly susceptible to the clever schemes which I put under their noses."

"Do I get this right?" asked a man who seemed more

intelligent than the rest. "You want to raid this 'college' to get hold of a drug which will destroy a man's sense of right and wrong?"

"Exactly!" said Boke.

"I'm with you," said the other.

Arguments and discussions followed, with some of the masterminds of crime holding out. But their reluctance was not too strong, and it was evident in a subtle way that Boke would win their aid.

Half an hour later, they entered the planes and took to the air.

When Doc Savage, Monk, Ham and Basenstein had flown over the area so strangely fenced off in the wilderness, there had been no sign of human life excepting the one man who had appeared at the log lodge near the gate.

There were fully two hundred men in sight now. They were all attired exactly alike in neat white uniforms, except for an individual here and there who was dressed in blue.

The men in white were arrayed in neat squads and were going through marches and physical-culture exercises, commanded by the men in blue. A few of the white garbed figures strolled about, obviously relaxing.

These men in white were former criminals, although their present appearance gave no indication of that fact. They were healthy, clear-eyed, and each was developing an excellent set of muscles. Not one of these men could remember any of his past life. Each could recall opening his eyes in a white room in this strange enclosure in the wilderness—that was all.

Over by the log lodge, which was not large enough to shelter a fraction of the men visible within the enclosure, a man was seated before a switchboard and an array of amplifiers: He wore an ordinary telephone headset, and was reading a late magazine.

Suddenly, he straightened, gave the amplifier knobs judicious turns, and an intent expression came over his face. He turned to another man, who was clad in the blue regalia.

"Listening device has picked up the sound of plane motors," he stated. "Sounds like two ships."

The other man went to a button, pressed it three times, and three great *donging* noises came from a gong concealed somewhere.

The results were miraculous. The men in white formed lines in doublequick time and marched for the hill of grayish rock. Doors opened in the apparently solid stone and the files of men streamed through and were lost to sight.

Within a very few minutes no one was left in sight in the whole fenced-in area.

The man at the listening post continued to wait. It was not often that airplanes passed over this remote region, but when they did, the patients at the strange 'college' were whisked from view. Due to the contour of the surrounding country, it was only from an airplane that the white-clad patients could be seen.

The planes appeared—two of them. The man at the listening post recognized Doc's big tri-motored craft, but the other ship was a stranger. The man went outside and semaphored a question with his arms.

His answer was a stream of machine-gun bullets which sent him racing wildly for shelter.

Possibly Boke considered the strange institution below one conceived only as a retreat where men's souls were remade and their lives altered, and, as such, a place without armament. He must not have known that Doc Savage, in planning the place, had foreseen the possible contingency of a gang of criminals trying to rescue one of their number from an unwelcome life of honesty.

There were many reasons why gangsters would want members of their tribe out of the place. So, as Boke suddenly discovered, thorough defense mechanism had been installed. This was the first time it had ever been used.

At numerous points, what looked like ordinary stretches of damp woodland loam slid back, uncovering neatly white-washed concrete gun pits. The weapons these housed were not large, nor were they toys, either. The gun muzzles lifted and began to follow the planes. This was uncanny, because there was no hand guiding the weapons in the pits.

Aiming was done by a blue-clad man at a concealed station. He simply sighted at one of the planes through a telescope which was attached to slides and cogs, and when he had crossed hairs on the craft, he pressed a lever.

The guns began firing. The man in the remote fire-control station turned a lever and the white puffs of bursting shells—they opened too high at first—crawled down toward the plane, not aiming at it, but ahead.

The aircraft, pummeled and rent by the metallic storm, banked away, but something had gone wrong with its power plant, and it labored along.

The pilot tried to climb, and discovered his control wires were damaged. He barely made it over the hill and into a feathery clump of evergreens, where he stalled away what speed he had and consigned himself to whatever goddess of luck that looks out for airmen, good or bad. And the goddess came through.

The plane lost its wings, undercarriage part of the empennage. The cabin went flat; small boughs pierced it. The noise was heard for two miles.

The pilot crawled out, picking glass parts of the instrument panel from his features, looked around and heaved a great sigh. Men were getting out of the wreckage, some more banged up than others, but it was evident they were all going to be able to walk away from it.

Overhead, the other plane circled. Boke was riding in that one, and it was evident that unexpected discovery that the "college" was a hornet's nest had temporarily discouraged him.

Chapter XVII

HARDBOILED'S MISTAKE

Doc Savage did not hear the roar as the plane crashed. But he did see the white fruit of bursting anti-aircraft shells which preceded the crack-up. And he caught the distant *pungs* as the shells exploded, although it was very faint.

The bronze man lay on the banks of the roaring stream, but not at the point where bullets had been rained from the planes. He was downstream.

There was a bullet hole through his Herculean torso. The slug, fortunately, had come from a rifle, and it had left a clean trail, entering his back at one side of the neck and angling down, doing something agonizing to a few bones, and coming out in the thick, magnificently developed pectoralis major muscle on the right side.

The bronze man carefully thrust his right hand inside his shirt, then got erect. He was clad only in shirt and underclothing.

He went up the stream and came to the spot where the planes had fired upon him. He examined the thing they had fired upon, thinking it was his body—a bundle composed of twigs and leaves and a few sticks, for stiffening purposes, thrust into his clothing. He had left it there under cover of the smoke, and as the wind swept the smoke toward the stream, had moved along with it and entered the cold water. The swim which followed was something he wished to forget.

Looking over the clothing, he found the coat so ripped as to be useless: the shoes, as well, had been torn badly by the bullets; but the trousers, under the coating of mud, were at least wearable. He donned them.

Then he headed for the "college."

The bronze man did not go as the crow flies, for only a crow or other aërial traveler could go that way; this country was not wilderness for no reason at all. It was primitive because it was almost impenetrable. The hills were sharp, multitudinous, and briars, thorny bushes and low brush made a mat which would vie with a tropical jungle.

The most simple route was to head south to the road, then follow that westward to the institution. Accordingly, Doc Savage turned south.

He reached the road. It was not graded, except where it of necessity had to be leveled off a bit; the bridges were of logs, and the whole affair smacked of the pioneer days. But it was passable by truck its whole length, and served to bring in heavy supplies which could not be carried handily by plane.

The woods still dripped; the breeze was making some noise, and the running streams kept up a wet orchestration. That possibly accounted for what happened next. Ordinarily, the bronze man was not taken unawares.

Ahead of him, a man stepped into the road. The fellow wore the uniform of a New York City policeman. He held a riot gun.

"We want to talk to you," he advised loudly.

Doc had stopped, and now he swung around slowly. More uniformed men had appeared on either side and at the rear. They numbered six—and a leader.

The leader was Inspector Clarence "Hardboiled" Humbolt. He alone was not in uniform, and he wore enormous overshoes and sheepskin pacs instead of his tennis shoes. But he still hobbled along as if his feet were raw stubs. Despite the feet, he looked as happy as a dog which had just caught a rabbit.

"We were afraid there wouldn't be a landing place up here for a plane," he rumbled. "So we left our ship at the last town and came on by car."

Doc Savage asked without emotion, "Have you any authority in this part of the State?"

Hardboiled shook the leather sap down out of his sleeve and swatted the palm of a corded hand with it.

"This is authority enough," he advised. "But I had the governor issue myself and my men special commissions before we left the big town."

Doc Savage shrugged. "Your man Basenstein seems to have balled things up," he said.

Hardboiled jumped as if some one had stepped on his tender feet. He peered owlishly at the bronze man.

"What's that?" he growled.

"Those notes Basenstein wrote you," Doc said. "They must have resulted in Boke and his gang following us up here."

Hardboiled swatted his palm with the sap, scowled, expectorated, and shifted from one foot to another. His features became dark with disgust.

"So I didn't fool you with Basenstein," he muttered.

"No," Doc told him. "But you might have, if I had not overheard you talking near Sidney Lorrey's barge laboratory. Basenstein told a good story. Just how much of it was the truth?"

"Most of it," Hardboiled grumbled reluctantly. "Sidney Lorrey did come to him to be treated, and he did talk a lot of stuff about the Crime Annihilist. He was either trying to say he was the Crime Annihilist himself, or, as I've been thinking later, he might have known who the Crime Annihilist was. Basenstein used to be a police medical examiner. He called me. I decided to put him on your trail."

"So I thought," Doc said dryly.

Hardboiled glared. "Why'd you let 'im hang around if you knew who he was?"

"He was," Doc said, "an excellent alibi."

Hardboiled swore. "Where's Basenstein?"

A policeman, a short distance down the road, yelled, "Hey! Look out, fellows!"

There was a shot. Doc and the others whirled. They were just in time to see the policeman running backward madly and waving his arms. The officer's heel hooked a bush and he went down so heavily that his heels flew up, then smacked back again; he coughed and a red spray went into the air.

From the dark woods a voice called, "Be good, coppers!"

Then other voices shouted from the sides, and it was evident that they were surrounded.

Hardboiled snarled, reached for his hip—and Doc Savage, grasping his arm, said, "You'll get your men killed!"

Two of the policemen dropped flat in the road, and for a moment it seemed there would be a fight; then the attackers circled and came out in the roads, their ready submachine guns discouraging the policemen.

"I know some of these mugs," Hardboiled gritted. "They're tough lads!"

The gunmen advanced, the officers were disarmed, then a slender man with a seamy face, who appeared to be in charge, relaxed and said, "Won't this tickle Boke!"

Doc Savage asked, "Will you tell me something?"

"No," said the man.

"What brought you up here?" Doc asked.

The man laughed. "Just about every time that Basenstein sent Hardboiled here a message, we either got it or got a look at it. Basenstein used the plane radio to tell Hardboiled where he had landed with you fellows, and we picked up the message."

Hardboiled looked very disgusted and tried to stand so as to ease his feet.

The man with the wizened face yelled. More gangsters came out of the woods, dragging two prisoners. The pig, Habeas, was with them.

Pat Savage was one of the captives; Renny was the other.

"We thought these might come in handy," smirked the gang lieutenant. "Come on. We'll go see how Boke is making out."

Boke, it was evident, was not making out in a manner satisfactory to himself. They could hear him swearing before they caught sight of him.

"*Tsk, tsk,*" Pat said. "That lad is no gentleman."

Two or three of Boke's men eyed Pat admiringly. They appreciated her nerve. Hardboiled scowled at her and demanded. "Don't you realize they're liable to kill all of us?"

Pat studied him as if trying to ascertain what made his temper bad, then decided aloud, "It must be your feet."

Boke came striding up and yelled, "Shut up! What is going on here? I thought this bronze man was dead!"

Some one told him about the capture.

"Excellent," shouted Boke. "We will take them all, rope them together and use them as a shield while we rush that gate."

Complying with that order, Monk and Ham were marched up and placed with Pat, Renny, Doc and the policemen. Shortly afterward, Basenstein arrived under escort and was confined to the collection.

"A fine spy *you* turned out to be," Hardboiled told him sarcastically.

"Well, that's gratitude," Basenstein snorted. "I hope you get bunions on your hands as well as on your feet!"

Hardboiled grinned in a way that showed he hadn't meant his criticism.

Boke confronted Doc Savage and announced, "You can save a lot of trouble by giving me the ingredients of the chemical which upsets this so-called crime gland. That's what I want."

The bronze man made no answer, seemed not to hear.

"Damn it!" Boke yelled. "Answer me!"

Doc Savage looked straight over Boke's head, saying nothing. From where he stood, he could see up the hill on which stood the cabin that was outside the fenced enclosure of the criminal "college"—perhaps a mile from the gate, although only about half a mile from where Doc now stood. The cabin looked very forlorn and deserted.

"Answer me!" Boke screeched.

Doc Savage said sharply, "You know your answer. What are you going to do about it?"

"Plenty!" Boke rapped, and turned away.

Some seventy yards distant, an evergreen shrub stirred slightly. A bit later, a stick broke. And after that, a bird flew up noisily from the side of the hill and sailed off in the direction of the cabin which stood alone.

Monk, speaking so that only Doc heard, asked, "Say, ain't there somebody skulking over there?"

"Yes," Doc said.

"Did you see who it was?" Monk demanded.

The bronze man shook a negative.

"Must be one of his gang," Monk hazarded.

"On the contrary," Doc said, "it is probably the Crime Annihilist."

Monk looked as if he were about to be upset. He scratched his jaw as best he could with his bound hands.

"Blazes!" he muttered. "You really think the guy is up here in person?"

"There is," Doc said, "not the slightest doubt of it."

Renny, who had shuffled over to hear the last, peered around cautiously, then eyed his big fists, which were purple from the tightness of the cords which confined them.

"How do you figure he's here, Doc?" he asked.

"The Crime Annihilist stopped working shortly after our plane appeared," said the bronze man. "It is logical to suppose that he saw our plane, feared we could trace him down, and shut off his device."

Monk grunted, "So that's why the thing quit working."

Up on the hill, another bird flushed up. This one was more distant, nearer the cabin.

"Whoever was hangin' around here is makin' for that cabin," Monk said abruptly.

Over toward the gate that led into the enclosure which held the fantastic "college," they could hear Boke yelling. He did not seem particularly anxious for a pitched battle, not knowing just what armament the fenced area held. He was demanding that the secret of the criminal-making drug be given to him, or he would start killing his prisoners.

"Is there such a drug, Doc?" Ham asked.

The bronze man nodded. "There is. The concoction was discovered in the course of experiments to learn how this so-called 'crime' gland could best be caused to function normally."

Their captors had tied all of them by now, securing their wrists, but leaving their ankles free, an ominous prediction of what was to come if worst turned to worst. Cotton rope had been used. The strands were thin and stout.

Most of the men departed to a spot from which the gate could be seen, anxious to learn how Boke's negotiations would turn out. Only four remained close to Doc Savage and the other prisoners, but they held submachine guns with the safeties latched off.

Doc Savage leaned against a tree as if weary, and worked an arm against the coarse bark. Unnoticed, a button came off his sleeve and fell to the ground. A moment later he sat down, as if his strength had given out. His fingers picked up the button.

It was white, as if constructed of ordinary pearl, but close examination would have shown that it was of metal and the edge, instead of being merely rounded, was disked to a razor sharpness. A thin metal band protected this edge, and was easily broken off with the finger nails, leaving the razor edge exposed.

Two or three judicious slices cut almost through Doc's wrist bonds.

He caught Monk's eye and flipped the button. Monk picked it up when the guards were not looking, kept a sober face as he discovered its purpose, used it and passed it on to Renny. Renny gave it to Pat, and Pat passed it to Ham.

Down by the gate, those inside the high fence had refused to have anything to do with Boke's demands.

Doc, pretending to writhe as though the pain from his shoulder were unbearable, dug his hands down into the ground and closed them over a stone which had been almost hidden in the mud.

"All right," he said suddenly, and flung the stone.

Simultaneously, Monk, Ham, Renny and Pat came to their feet.

The flung rock, taking a machine gunner by surprise, dropped him trembling in his tracks. The other three gunmen, amazed, squawled out an alarm and tried to get their weapons into play.

Monk, reaching one, swung a fist as if he were driving a nail, and the man went down.

Two of the others got their rapidfirers chattering, but had no time to aim before Ham and Renny were upon them. Renny clubbed his man down with slamming blows. Ham had a little trouble until Pat, running around behind, rabbit-punched the gangster. Ham finished him off with an uppercut. The pig, Habeas, began squealing.

"Get their guns!" Doc rapped. "And retreat up the hill!"

Monk yelled, "Listen, there ain't nothing but that cabin at the top of the hill! No place to hole up! Why not try to get over the fence?"

"Up the hill!" Doc repeated, and began untying Hardboiled Humbolt and the other policemen.

Hardboiled bellowed, "Ain't you gonna fight them mugs?"

Doc said; "Get up that hill! Make for the cabin!"

"Why not fight 'em?" Hardboiled howled.

"Because some of them might be killed!" Doc rapped. "Get a move on!"

The fugitives were stringing out up the hill, and a few bullets were snapping through the timber in pursuit. Due to the thickness of the woods, the slugs were poorly aimed.

Hardboiled, hopping along painfully with a disgruntled look, drew up beside Renny and demanded, "What's eatin' that bronze guy? Why don't he fight them birds? We could knock off about half of 'em with them Tommy guns."

"Matter of principle," Renny rumbled. "Doc never kills anybody."

"Hell!" said Hardboiled. "Killin' is too good for Boke and that crowd!"

"Shut up and run," Renny advised. "I don't know why Doc is makin' for that cabin, but he has some reason."

The bronze man was not leading the retreat, but bringing up the rear. From time to time, he discharged a burst from one of the captured submachine guns, but he shot high, merely discouraging the rapidity of pursuit.

It became evident that they were going to reach the cabin before they were overhauled. Monk was carrying his pet pig.

Hardboiled, reaching the cabin finally, ran around it and looked down the slope beyond.

"Hell's bells!" he roared. "We're stuck!"

The hill sloped gently; there was little underbrush which would furnish shelter; and the tree trunks themselves were thin, none being greater than six inches in diameter.

Doc Savage paid no attention. He was studying the wet ground before the cabin. It bore fresh tracks. Some of the prints were so recent that they were still filling with water, and they had been made by the same pair of feet, judging from their likeness in size.

The bronze man mounted to a creaking porch and shoved inside. The room was large, roughly furnished, the principal fixture being a large bench strewn with wires, bits of metal and vacuum tubes of diverse design.

Across the room was a closed door. A voice came from behind it.

"Get away from me!" it shrilled.

Monk, diving into the cabin behind Doc, let his jaw sag down, then snapped it up to demand wonderingly, "Who in blazes is in that room?"

"The Crime Annihilist, I believe," Doc said.

"Well, well," Monk grunted, and dived across the room. He hit the door with his shoulder, and his homely face showed that he fully expected it to collapse. But he was too optimistic. The stout wooden panel held.

"Get away!" shrieked the voice from the other side of the door.

Then a roar of gunfire and a snapping and crashing of bullets drowned out the shrieks. Nearly all of the glass fell out of the room's one window. It jingled not unmusically on the floor.

Ham, Pat, Hardboiled and all the policemen were inside.

"Get down," Doc directed. "The logs will turn lead."

Monk, seeming unaware of the danger outside, jabbed a thumb at the inner room into which they had not yet had time to smash their way.

"How'd you know the Crime Annihilist was here?" he demanded.

"Direction finding apparatus," Doc said. "I used it from New York City."

"You mean——"

"That this Crime Annihilist's weapon is merely a machine emitting emanations similar to ultra-short radio waves," Doc said. "These emanations have an irritating effect on the so-called 'crime' gland, causing a sort of local poisoning which induces mental spasms and a peculiar muscular reaction which results in the protruding of the eyes."

"You'll have to make it clearer than that for me to get it," Monk grunted.

"I used a sensitive directional finder of an ordinary radio type, in the New York laboratory," Doc went on. "It pointed to this vicinity."

Monk exploded, "Now listen, Doc—that's a bit thick. No directional device would point to this cabin."

"It pointed in this direction," Doc corrected. "The rest was guesswork. This cabin was the logical spot."

Monk began, "I don't see——" then fell silent. He wet his lips, flattened a little lower as a bullet ricocheted down from the ceiling.

"Blazes!" he exploded. "This cabin was built——"

Hardboiled Humbolt interrupted, bawling, "Hey! Lookit! Lookit!"

And the shooting stopped as if it had only been some recorded sound effect which had been switched off.

Silence did not fall. Rather, the shooting stopped and a banshee caterwauling of shouts took its place. The shouts became screams, and these turned to awful shrieks.

They were all conscious of a metallic drone which had started up and seemed to be coming from the adjacent room.

Pat ran to the window, broken glass crunching under her feet. She looked out only briefly, then withdrew, hands lifting in a subconscious gesture of horror. Her face looked drained, drawn.

"The Crime Annihilist!" she said thickly. "They're dying outside! The thing seems to be stronger than ever before."

Doc Savage got erect and flung himself against the door of the room from which the drone came. The panel rebuffed him as it had Monk. He hit it again, using his unwounded shoulder. He picked up a chair and battered it, and the sound this produced told him why the door was so solid.

"Metal lined," he said. "Probably a storeroom!"

The bronze man ran to the workbench, dumped its litter and tore at one of the great, thick planks which composed its top.

"Give us a hand!" he rapped. "We've got to get into this inside room to save those men out there."

Monk, who was usually prompt in carrying out the bronze man's suggestions, for once seemed not to hear. Monk, at times in the past, had been suspected of possessing bloodthirsty inclinations. He looked through the window, grimaced, but did not turn away.

The sight was not a pleasant one to watch. Boke's men had worked quite close to the cabin when the affliction seized them; from the window, Monk had a box seat for the pageant of fantastic death.

The homely chemist located Janko Sultman. He had already succumbed, and was a contorted shape beneath a tree. A strange thing had happened to his frizzled hair as death overtook him. The hair was no longer upstanding, but lay down as if it, too, had been devoid of life.

Monk discovered Boke. The mastermind had been well behind, out of danger of bullets, a position masterminds not infrequently occupy. But it had not preserved him from the vengeance of the Crime Annihilist.

Boke was stumbling about, shrieking, beating at his own face. He tore off the muffler which had masked his features, then fell to the ground, stretched himself out and did not move again.

Monk craned his neck to get a closer look at Boke's face. Monk snorted. It was not a face of a leader. It had fragile features and a rose petal skin. No hardboiled crook would look upon such a face and feel like calling its owner his master. It was no mystery why Boke had kept his face covered.

For Boke was the feminine-mannered Lizzie. Probably Janko Sultman had never known that, and it explained how Sultman had been discovered in his double-crossing. For Lizzie had ostensibly been one of Sultman's gang.

Several men clutched the long plank which Doc had ripped from the workbench. They drew back, leveled it and ran for the door in a living ram. The panel gave, groaned. A second smash caused it to give slightly more. With a roar it went in on the third try.

Doc Savage pitched across the threshold. The room beyond was dark, for there were no windows. But there was a furtive movement in a corner. The bronze man squinted through the murk.

"Get back!" he rapped suddenly. Then he lunged forward.

In a remote corner, a figure was huddled over a mound of objects on the floor. The figure straightened, gibbering shrilly, as the bronze man approached.

Doc swooped upon the objects over which the figure had been crouched. There was dynamite, nearly a case of it, with a battery and wires attached; there was also a small phonograph, one of the type newly placed on the market which can be plugged into a light circuit and, by using a microphone attachment, employed to make records, which can then be played back numerous times.

Doc hastily disconnected the wires from the explosive, while the occupant of the room squeaked meaninglessly at him from across the chamber.

Monk came lumbering in, Renny on his heels. They looked at the pitiful figure which was the Crime Annihilist.

"Holy cow!" Renny boomed.

And Monk, pointing at the explosive, the phonograph, said, "That's how he faked his death on the barge. Got away before we ever came, and left a rifle attached to the door so that it would go off when the door was jarred. Then he had the phonograph yell out in his voice, and then the explosion. He was fixing to do the same thing here."

Monk shook his head slowly, then resumed: "But why?"

Ham, who had come in, said caustically, "You ape, if you had been through what he has, you would do queer things too."

Then they looked at the Crime Annihilist, at his racked body, a frame mutilated by torture, swathed in bandages, and it was not difficult to understand why he had set out to rid the world of criminals.

"They killed my brother!" mumbled the Crime Annihilist. "Damn them—they—they—I'll get them all!"

The Crime Annihilist was Sidney Lorrey.

Chapter XVIII

MONK TAKES HIS DAY

The opposite wall of the room was spanned its full length by a table, and on this was arrayed a tremendous quantity of electrical apparatus. Under the table, a motor-generator set made a metallic drone.

"The thing that produced the pop-eyed death," Ham murmured, and eyed the array.

Doc Savage nodded.

"Sidney Lorrey was—is—a scientist and surgeon interested in mental therapy as influenced by various infra-rays and light beams," the bronze man said. "I recall Robert Lorrey saying that Sidney was trying to perfect a treatment for the so-called 'crime' gland which would not require the use of drugs."

The bronze man indicated the intricate array of electrical apparatus. "Possibly Sidney Lorrey did not realize at first that his apparatus was killing criminals. It must have been set up in his barge laboratory and operating continuously on some piece of experimental tissue. Then, when Sidney saw the men die from its effects, he realized what it was."

"And realized what a weapon against crime he had," Ham added.

Monk pointed at Sidney Lorrey. "What about him?"

Doc Savage went over to Sidney Lorrey. The latter recoiled at first, but under the bronze man's soothing words, submitted to an examination.

"Temporarily disarranged mentally by pain," Doc said. "He will be entirely normal after a short period of treatment and a rest."

Monk muttered slowly, "I'm glad of that."

Hardboiled Humbolt was moving about as if he had something on his mind, but was uncertain what to do about it. He caught Doc Savage's eye and beckoned. They went out on the porch.

Hardboiled waved an arm in the direction of the area of woodland enclosed by the high fence.

"What's over there?" he demanded. "You've got somethin' up here, somethin' big. I ain't quite been able to figure out what it is."

Doc Savage studied the big, rough-mannered cop for some moments.

"That, to put it plainly, was a lie," he said dryly. "From Boke's talk, you secured a very good idea of what is inside that fence."

Hardboiled shook his head. "I didn't hear a thing."

Doc Savage extended a hand. "Thanks. If news of that place got out, it would mean all kinds of trouble."

"I got a few special friends." Hardboiled jerked his hand at the criminal-curing institution again. "Would you put 'em in there—when I catch 'em? Just as a favor?"

The bronze man rarely smiled, but he did so now. "With pleasure," he agreed.

Hardboiled asked, "What are you gonna do about that thing inside—that mess of electrical business?"

"Destroy it," Doc said.

"Why?" Hardboiled looked pained. "Think of what it'd do to the crooks!"

Doc Savage asked, "When a man has the smallpox, do you kill him?"

"Hell, no!" Hardboiled snorted. "You doctor him up."

"Exactly!" Doc Savage said. "And that explains why I am going to destroy the device inside."

The bronze man picked up a fragment of the chair with which he had first tried to batter down the door, and entered the inner room. He ran his eyes over the assembled apparatus of the Crime Annihilist until he had the circuit fixed in his memory.

It might become useful sometime in the future.

He shut off the motor-generator, then went to work with the piece of chair, smashing tubes, tearing apart intricate bundles of wires. The vacuum tubes broke with loud explosions, showering glass about. Delicate insulating sheets crunched, and condensers, torn apart, spilled layers of foil and waxed paper.

Doc did the job of destruction carefully, expending fully five minutes in the task, and when he was done and had stepped back, Monk thrust his homely features into the room. He pointed at the apparatus, or what was left of it.

"Is that jigger out of whack?" he demanded.

"It is," Doc told him.

Monk licked his lips. A look of unholy anticipation came over his features, and he retreated from the door.

It could not have been more than thirty seconds later when a terrific scream ripped out. It was followed by growls, minor howls, and the thump and bang of a terrific fight.

Ham, his coat and most of his shirt missing, the rest of his person looking as if it had been through a tornado, dashed madly around a cabin corner.

Monk popped out in pursuit, still gripping parts of Ham's missing clothing.

"Help!" Ham yelled. "Turn that blasted machine on!"

"What they're gonna have to turn on for you," Monk puffed grimly, "is slow music!"